Just Leave Us
Alone!

Just Leave Us Alone!

RICHARD SLOANE

Just Leave Us Alone!

Copyright © 2024 by Richard Sloane. All rights reserved.

No part of this publication may be reproduced, stored in a retrieval system or transmitted in any way by any means, electronic, mechanical, photocopy, recording or otherwise without the prior permission of the author except as provided by USA copyright law.

The opinions expressed by the author are not necessarily those of URLink Print and Media.

1603 Capitol Ave., Suite 310 Cheyenne, Wyoming USA 82001
1-888-980-6523 | admin@urlinkpublishing.com

URLink Print and Media is committed to excellence in the publishing industry.

Book design copyright © 2024 by URLink Print and Media. All rights reserved.

Published in the United States of America

Library of Congress Control Number: 2024910011
ISBN 978-1-68486-769-1 (Paperback)
ISBN 978-1-68486-772-1 (Digital)

07.05.24

Contents

Chapter 1 7
Chapter 2 11
Chapter 3 14
Chapter 4 19
Chapter 5 23
Chapter 6 27
Chapter 7 31
Chapter 8 34
Chapter 9 38
Chapter 10... 43
Chapter 11 49
Chapter 12 58
Chapter 13 66
Chapter 14... 73
Chapter 15 82
Chapter 16... 87
Chapter 17... 91
Chapter 18 95
Chapter 19 104
Chapter 20 109
Chapter 21 114
Chapter 22 117
Chapter 23 125
Chapter 24... 131
Chapter 25 144
Chapter 26... 152
Chapter 27... 156
Chapter 28 163
Chapter 29 171

Chapter

1

Not much had happened during the past ten years since Gwendolyn, the fairy queen, and Titan, the leprechaun king, had managed to get the airport moved to another location. However, that was soon to change.

Always hanging over the fairies' and leprechauns' heads was the potential threat of their existence becoming known to humans being exposed in spite of the fact that they had a supposedly watertight agreement signed by the Attorney General himself giving them their forest forever. But nobody had accounted for a clerical error in the filing of this document which was supposed to have said that it could not be declassified for a minimum of 100 years. Unfortunately, however, the clerk who had typed up this instruction had missed off the final 0 in the time frame so that it read as if it could be declassified in 10 years. And this is what happened.

An investigative reporter, called Damien Fletcher, who worked for one of the big Dublin newspapers, knew that declassified documents often had secrets buried within them which, even after 10 years, could be written about. He was diligently reading through these documents when he came across one which made him sit bolt upright. It said that that a forest in the west of Ireland (and it gave its geographical coordinates) was *'deeded to its 'indigenous inhabitants' in perpetuity'*, which Damien knew meant that the land would be left to them forever. But what 'indigenous inhabitants' was it talking about? So he took a quick photocopy of the document.

He felt in his bones that here was a career-making story but, before he rushed off to his editor with it, he knew he had to do more research. So first he left his office and went to the public library where he looked up the coordinates on a large scale map and quickly found the forest referred to. It appeared to be very isolated with only a few small hamlets nearby. Next he looked up stories from the region in as many newspapers as he could find from ten years before and saw that an airport had been scheduled to be built in this forest but, after a few weeks' work, this was mysteriously moved to another site some 25 miles north.

He could feel his excitement building but there was one more thing he needed to do and, for that, he needed a powerful computer, preferably one with satellite access. But then he remembered a popular mapping website and wondered whether the forest had been scanned by them. He knew that they covered most of the earth's surface, especially the built-up areas and wanted to see if he could spot any of these mysterious 'indigenous inhabitants'.

So he ran back to his office and powered up his computer again before going into the website and entering the forests' coordinates. And he was very pleasantly surprised when up came a video of the forest taken by a satellite hundreds of miles overhead. He saw that the video was about half an hour long so he settled into his comfortable office chair and prepared to view the pictures. It was clearly night time because the camera was using infra red.

But after 10 minutes with only lots of trees to see, he was starting to get bored when suddenly he noticed that the satellite was passing over a large clearing near the centre of the forest and he asked the computer to slow right down. It was showing a lot of strange shapes on the ground which were perfectly round, of different sizes, and apparently made of some kind of vegetation. He had never seen anything like them before but he would have sworn that they weren't made by animals but by some kind of higher intelligence. So he asked the computer to zoom in and print out a few stills of these – dwellings, maybe? He was disappointed that there didn't seem to be any videos online taken in the day time but he knew he couldn't have everything.

Then, armed with his pictures and notes, he ran upstairs to his editor's office and barged straight in. His editor, an older lady called Luella, looked up from some papers she was signing and said, sighing, 'Why don't you learn to knock, Damien? But now you're here, what can I do for you?'

'I think I might be on to something!' Damien said breathlessly.

'Do go on,' Luella said. Damien just happened to be one of her up-and-coming star reporters and she knew that she ignored these hunches of his at her peril.

'I was going through some declassified documents and came across this,' Damien said, passing her the photocopy of the original document. She read it through slowly and then said, 'Yes, I agree it's interesting. And I know what you're going to say next. Who are these 'indigenous inhabitants' that are mentioned?'

Damien replied, somewhat deflated at her having taken the wind out of his sails, 'Yes, exactly. So I did some research.' And he told her about everything he had done so far. When he'd finished, he said, 'And this is what I came up with!' and he presented her with the stills pictures of the clearing in the forest which she looked at for a few seconds. Then he just sat back and waited for her verdict.

'My, you have been a busy bee, haven't you?' Luella said before continuing, 'but I think you're going to need to do more research before you go rushing off to the wilds of nowhere. Specifically, I'd like you to find out what you can about this airport. I happen to know that the old Attorney General is now dead as is Mr Doggett, the planning Minister, to all intents and purposes, the two signatories to your document. At least I heard that he was put into a nursing home for patients with advanced senile dementia. So you probably need to find out who else was involved in the airport and go and interview them.'

Damien recognised the wisdom in her words and said, 'Yes, OK. Will do. Anything else? I think time is pretty tight though. I'm worried about the competition.'

'No. I think that's everything for the moment. And don't worry about them. I'm sure you're ahead of the game. Keep me informed.'

'Yes, ma'am!' And he left her office on a high, knowing he had her backing.

Chapter

2

Damien was the son of a newspaper man himself – his father had worked on a provincial paper all his life – and after studying journalism at university near his home town, he went to the capital to seek his fortune and was lucky to find a job pretty much straight away. He rose quickly in the ranks as he was a quick-witted young man, and, after a few years, applied for a job at his present prestigious paper as an investigative reporter. He was turned down the first time but this didn't deter him and he tried again after a few more months and this time was successful. He actually took over the post of an elderly journalist who had just retired. This was the ideal job for him and he thrived, hunting down the stories, often in his own time. He also got married to a lady called Moira, now that he felt secure in a decent job.

But that's enough about his background. The relevance of this to the present account was that he was a true child of Ireland, steeped in all its old legends. Indeed, the first book he ever managed to read completely was a child's storybook about leprechauns and it really captured his imagination. And from then on he read everything he could find on these supposedly mythical creatures. He often wondered to himself if it could be possible that leprechauns or something like them could still exist in the distant wilds of his country. And here, presented to him on a plate, was possibly the answer to his question. He didn't mention this to Luella as he didn't want to be laughed out of court but he wondered if his wise, old editor had intuited that he had a personal interest in this story or even if she wondered the same thing he did.

Anyway, he knew he had to get on and do the research she had asked for. So, after he got back to his office, he looked up the number of the new airport and, after presenting his credentials, asked for somebody who knew the history of it. And, as luck would have it, he got put through to a lady who was very helpful. She had been there from the very beginning, she told him, and when he asked her for the name of the developer, she went away and looked it up for him. It was a Mr McManus, one of the biggest property developers in the country, a name he'd heard before, as he'd seen a profile of him in a business magazine not long before.

Then he told her he'd seen a news article in a local paper about a previous location for the airport and asked her why the location had been changed at the last minute. She said there was some mystery about that but that she'd always presumed that it was simply because the present location was more convenient for the city as it had been built on land already owned by the Council and McManus wouldn't have had to pay private landowners for their property. He thanked her very much for her help and said he might get back to her if he had any more questions.

After that he hung up and went back up to his editor and told her what he'd found out and she said that obviously he needed to get an interview with McManus. He agreed and, as always when he was on the trail of a story, decided that he needed more background on McManus before interviewing him, so he went to the newspaper's extensive library and looked up stories about him. He quickly discovered that he was pretty ruthless about getting his contracts but it was all hearsay, nothing concrete that he could actually use against him. He also read the magazine profile and discovered that he lived in Dublin with his wife in a big old house near the sea in one of the most desirable neighbourhoods of the city.

Next he rang the headquarters of McManus' business empire and asked if he could speak to his private secretary and, when he got her on the line, asked, after giving his credentials again, if she could organise an appointment with her boss. And she, knowing McManus' love of the limelight, said yes, she didn't see why not. He thanked her effusively and asked if it could be as soon as possible as he was under a strict deadline from his editor. So she looked up McManus' diary and said, 'How about tomorrow morning? He happens to be around at the moment.'

'That would be perfect!' he enthused and they agreed on 11 o'clock at McManus' office in the city centre. He didn't tell his editor about the appointment as he didn't want to keep bothering her and instead busied himself finishing off an article she'd asked for. Then he tidied his desk and, making sure he had all the documents he needed for the next morning in his briefcase, especially the strange contract which had started the whole thing, he just drove home. There his wife and 18-month-old daughter, Sophie, were surprised and pleased to find him home so early as he usually worked very long hours.

He played with his daughter before putting her to bed, all the while musing about how easy it had been so far and worrying about the interview the next day. Then he just had an almost silent dinner with his wife, who knew his moods, guessing he was onto a big story and not disturbing his train of thought, before going to bed himself.

Chapter 3

When he got up the next morning, he felt rested at least and not so worried about the interview. He shaved carefully, putting on his best suit – the one he hadn't worn since the interview for his present job – as he didn't mix much with the high society in the city, usually only seeing the ordinary people, and a clean white shirt but he still refused to wear a tie. When he went downstairs for breakfast with his wife and daughter, she took one look at him and said, 'Got an important interview coming up then?' guessing the situation correctly. 'Yes, potentially,' he replied but refused to answer any more questions.

Then, breakfast finished, he kissed his wife and Sophie goodbye and waved them off, his wife going to drop the baby at child care before going on to the big hospital where she worked as a midwife. After that he settled down to read the morning papers but didn't see anything which was relevant to him and he just hoped that Luella's comment about him being ahead of the game with his competitors was true. He'd already calculated how long it would take him to get to McManus' office and, when he looked at his watch, he reckoned he could leave now as he didn't know how long it would take him to find a parking spot. So he locked the house, put his briefcase on the back seat and drove slowly there.

In fact, it was easy to park when he got there as the company had its own car park in the basement. It was in the centre of the commercial district and when he walked through the big revolving doors, he noticed at once the tastefulness of the decor with large photos of some of McManus' biggest developments on the walls. He walked across the foyer to a receptionist and said with a smile, 'I have an appointment to see Mr McManus at 11 o'clock. My name's Damien Fletcher.'

She looked back at him, gave him a big smile back and said, 'Oh yes, Mr Fletcher, you're expected. Go on up to the top floor and his secretary will meet you at the lift,' gesturing to where it was. He thanked her and strolled over to where she'd pointed. He got in and pressed the button for the top of the building, noticing how many floors there were and thinking that that this really was a big operation and feeling a little intimidated now. 'Come on, Damien. Remember who you work for,' he thought, the words making him immediately feel better.

McManus' secretary, an older woman, was indeed there to meet him and she asked him first for his credentials which he presented with a flourish. She compared the photo of him on his official Press accreditation with his face before passing it back to him, saying, 'One can't be too careful these days.' 'Very true,' he replied. Then she led him down a deserted corridor to what was obviously her office outside a pair of imposing double doors with a couple of comfortable armchairs in it. 'Do sit down, Mr Fletcher,' she said. 'I'll see if he's free yet.' And she picked up a telephone on her desk and said, 'Mr Fletcher's here, sir.' Damien heard a deep voice say, 'Wheel him in, Mrs O'Leary.' He looked at his watch, saw he was 8 minutes early and intuited from that that McManus was probably a man who was keen on keeping good relations with the Press, an advantage for him.

He went into a vast corner office with a spectacular view of the city all the way down to the glittering sea with a large desk at one end, covered with papers, and a large man sitting behind it, probably in his early sixties, with a big thick mane of white hair and a craggy, weather-beaten face. There was a long sofa at one end of the office opposite the desk with a coffee table in front of it and he got up now and came round to where Damien was standing just inside the door. He shook hands with him and Damien noticed that he had a strong grip. He was a couple of inches shorter than Damien and looked in good shape. He ushered him to the sofa and then said, 'Can I get you anything?'

'I wouldn't say no to a cup of coffee,' Damien replied.

'How do you take it?' McManus asked.

'Just a little milk, please. No sugar.'

Then McManus went outside and Damien heard him give his secretary the order, using the short break to make sure his precious photocopy was in the inside pocket of his jacket. When McManus came back in, he sat at the other end of the sofa and said, 'Now what can I do for you, young man?'

'I'd just like a little background on a few of your business successes. But first, this is a beautiful building. Did you design it yourself?' thinking that a little flattery never went amiss and already knowing the answer.

'No but one of my architects did with some input from me. Thank you for the compliment. I like it.'

Now that the ice had been broken, Damien decided to head cautiously into more dangerous waters. 'I really wanted to ask you something about the airport you built about 10 years ago in the far west. Why did you put it where you did?'

'Oh, that's an easy question to answer. It lies on Council owned land which was very convenient for us as it meant that we didn't have to pay out a fortune to local landowners for their property. It made economic sense.'

At that moment his secretary came in bearing a silver tray with a couple of cups of steaming coffee on it and a plate of biscuits. 'Thank you, Mrs O'Leary,' he said and Damien thanked her as well. Then after she'd left, Damien took a sip and said appreciatively, 'Mmm. Good coffee.'

'We like to look after our visitors.'

'Yes, I can see that,' Damien replied before adding, 'and yes, I appreciate what you just said about not paying the local landowners.' Then he decided that was enough pussy-footing around and said, 'But I believe that you started building the airport in a different location. Is that a common occurrence?'

'Yes. I did and no it's not but it can happen on occasion. You're well informed.'

'Thank you,' Damien said now. But then, like a magician pulling a rabbit out of a hat, he took the photocopy of the contract out of his pocket and passed it over to McManus, asking as he did so, 'How do you account for this then?'

He saw McManus read it and he could have sworn the older man went white with shock before he whispered, 'Where the hell did you get this?' This was a reaction that Damien hadn't predicted.

'It was declassified yesterday.'

'They promised me it would stay secret for at least a hundred years,' he said even more quietly now.

'Well, I'm afraid the cat's out of the bag now. I really wanted to ask you about the so-called 'indigenous inhabitants' it mentions. Who are they?'

'I'm afraid I can't talk to you about that. Now I think you'd better leave.'

'Are you sure you don't want to talk to me? After all, I'm on your side at the moment.'

'Yes, I'm sure. Just go, please.'

'OK but don't forget that, if I find any evidence of wrong-doing on your part, I'm bound by law to tell the authorities.'

'Good luck with that,' McManus said now, waving him out and looking very worried. And that was that. He left, thinking about all the secrets out there in society and McManus' strange reaction to the document.

Chapter 4

Damien knew that he had to go back now and tell Luella about the interview and he drove slowly back to the office, trying to remember every word of the short conversation. When he got in, he made a few notes before going up to see his boss. He remembered to knock this time and when she replied, he went in to find her ensconced with a couple of the lower level editors who she at once shooed out to leave him alone with her.

'I went to see McManus this morning,' he began and then proceeded to tell her everything that had transpired. She listened quietly, not interrupting, and he finished by saying, 'If that's not strange, I don't know what is.'

She said, 'I picked up particularly on one thing, the words, *'They promised me it would stay secret for at least 100 years.'* Are you sure those were his exact words?'

'Yes, I'm sure. Those were his exact words and I honestly thought he was going to faint from sheer shock when he saw the contract.'

'Well, if that's true, it looks as if you've accessed some information which was supposed to be kept secret for a lot longer than it was.'

'Yes, I know. But I hope that's not going to stop me from writing the story, if there is one.'

'No, I don't think so although I'll have to talk to our lawyers about that, but I think it might work to our advantage. I'll get on to the government's Department of Records and find out what happened. If it turns out he was right and there's been some sort of error made, I'm sure they will immediately reclassify it and, provided that none of your competitors have got the information yet, it means you should have a clear field to do more research.'

'Are you telling me that I can now go to the forest and check it out with your blessing?'

'Yes, I don't see why not.'

Damien gave a whoop of joy when she said that and left her office on a real high. He now had to think about all the preparations he had to make for his trip, not least about telling his wife he had to go away. He had been prepared to go anyway, without Luella's sanction, spending his own money on the trip and taking the rest of his annual holiday to do it, but now that she had approved it, he wouldn't have to spend any of his own money, which was a big relief. He wasn't a wealthy man.

He hoped he could leave within the next couple of days while the weather was still reasonable and the first thing he did when he got back to his own office was to check out the flights from the capital to the nearest airport to the forest. This turned out to be the new one McManus had built and he quickly found out that planes left twice a week, with the next one scheduled for three days' time. He bought a ticket on this flight and also hired a car for when he got there, keeping the receipts for his expenses later.

Then he looked up the pubs local to the forest on the internet, hoping that he might be able to stay in one of them, and, on telephoning a couple of them quickly found one that looked very nice and that had B & B facilities. So he booked a room saying that he wasn't sure how long he'd be staying. The receptionist said that was fine, telling him just that they'd take his credit card details when he arrived.

He hung up thinking that he'd just completed a very successful morning but when he looked at his watch, he realised it was already 3.00 pm and he was very hungry. So he went out to a local pub frequented by many of his colleagues and ordered a decent lunch which he ate with relish.

Then it was back to the office where he rang up to Luella and told her when he was leaving. He also let her know that he wasn't sure when he'd be back but he thought it wouldn't be more than about a week. He added that he would make sure that he had cleared his desk completely of work before he left.

She listened to all this and said, 'Keep in touch and good luck! I'm very interested in this story.'

Then he simply went home where his wife and daughter had also just arrived. He told her that he had to go away on Saturday in three days for a bit for work.

'What does a bit mean?' she asked.

'I'm not sure but it shouldn't be more than a week.'

'And where are you going?'

'To a very remote part of the island in the far west. And before you ask, yes, I may be onto something very big, possibly the biggest story I've ever dealt with, although it may be nothing at all.'

She sighed and said, 'As long as it's not more than a week, that should be ok. Can you tell me anything else?'

'I'd rather not. My editor is the only one who knows the details and even she doesn't know what I'm suspecting. But I'll keep in touch every day, I promise.'

'All very mysterious then,' she said but left it there and he went up to her and gave her a big kiss, saying, 'Thanks for being so understanding.'

After supper he put the baby to bed and watched some mindless TV on the sofa with Moira before going to bed himself.

Chapter 5

The next three days passed in a whirlwind of activity, finishing his work, fending off his colleagues' curious questions about where he was going and deciding what to take with him. Luella told him that she'd been in touch with the Department of Records and that McManus was right and that the mistake was down to human error. They were very grateful for her bringing it to their attention and said the contract would be reclassified immediately.

And, before he knew it, he was waiting in line at the airport. He had been wondering, if everything worked out, whether there might be a book in the story. Like most journalists, he was jealous of people who had actually published books and longed to do so himself. So he decided, while he was waiting for the plane, to keep extensive notes of everything that had happened so far on his laptop and this kept him busy until he disembarked.

His plane was on time and when he arrived at the airport, which he had never been to before, he quickly found the car hire place and soon found himself on the road to the city. He passed straight through it, heading south, and then headed out into the wilds of the countryside. And it really was wild! He was a city lad at heart and he didn't know this part of the country at all but the sun was shining and he recognised the beauty of the countryside.

At last he reached the hamlet he was looking for and found the pub where he was to stay and it looked even nicer than it had on the internet. There was actually another reason why he wanted to stay at a pub: he hoped he might find some oldies who could give him some information about whether or not there were really leprechauns living in the forest nearby as he guessed that they would be his best sources. He had brought plenty of Euros to grease palms if he had to and knew that a pint of Guinness or an Irish whisky was probably the best way to get any information they had.

He'd told the receptionist on the phone that he was a journalist but that he was simply trying to get out of the city and do some walking. So it was partly true. That first night, however, he didn't meet any likely candidates, in spite of buying a round of drinks for the table at which he was sitting. But he knew he had plenty of time and didn't push it and, after dinner, he simply went up to his room, rang Moira, made a few more notes on his laptop and went to bed.

The next morning it looked like rain and after breakfast Damien put on his walking clothes and boots and went out to scout around. He'd done his research and knew where the forest was so he headed off in that direction. It was about a 4 mile trek along little roads where he didn't meet anybody at all until he came to a big path which he presumed would take him to the area where the first airport was scheduled to have been built.

It was very muddy here but he was wearing suitable boots and didn't mind. And, quite soon, he reached what appeared to be a very long fence with beyond it a thick forest. There was a gate leading inside but it was closed and heavily padlocked. He knew he would have no chance of entering here so he walked along the perimeter of the fence in both directions although he didn't make it as far as the ocean, but there didn't seem to be any breaks in it at all where he could enter and, as it was now raining quite heavily, he decided to simply turn around and go back to the pub.

Once he got there, he took off of his wet rainproof gear and went back down to the bar. And this time word seemed to have got around about a generous stranger who was prepared to buy people drinks and there were several tables of oldies, all sipping their pints of ale. He was hungry now after his long walk and decided to have a quick lunch before doing some more canvassing for information. When he'd eaten alone at a table, he got up and strolled over to one of the tables where some of the oldies were sitting.

'Can I buy any of you a drink?' he asked.

'You certainly can, young man,' one of them said, proffering him his empty glass. He was quickly followed by the other three at the table and Damien took all the empty glasses over to the bar and got them refilled. Then he sat down at the table where another chair had appeared.

'Cheers!' he said, clinking glasses with the old-timers.

'What's your name?' one of them said.

'Damien. What are yours?' And there were introductions all round.

'We hear you're from the capital on holiday?' another of them said in his broad rural accent.

'Yes, you're absolutely right. You're well informed,' he replied, sipping his ale.

'What's happening there? We're a bit cut off out here,' another of them said. And Damien regaled them with some choice gossip he'd heard from some of his colleagues which made them all laugh. Then he decided to go for broke and asked a question of his own.

'I was told on the way here that there was a tribe of leprechauns living in the forest nearby. Is this true?'

The oldies looked at one another for a moment, looking a bit discomfited by the question, until one of them replied, 'We don't talk about them, I'm afraid.'

'I'm so sorry. I didn't mean to embarrass you. It's just my natural curiosity. Let's change the subject,' Damien said, doing just that by asking them what it was like living in a small hamlet and quickly managed to get them back on his side but inwardly he was cheering, knowing that they had all but confessed to his suspicions. He bought another round of drinks, said bye to his new mates and left the bar, feeling well pleased with his afternoon's work.

He went up to his room and continued making notes on his laptop. Then he rang Luella and told her he was making good progress and hopefully should have something more concrete to tell her by the end of the next day. After that he looked out of his window and saw it was still raining and decided to have a nap. He woke up a couple of hours later, when it was getting dark, and decided that there was nothing more he could do that day so he read a book he'd brought with him until supper time and he could ring his wife. Then it was just a question of having a quick dinner, watching the news on TV, making some sort of plan for the next day and going to bed.

Chapter

6

He didn't sleep very well that night, whether because he'd had the long nap the day before or because he was excited about the coming day, he wasn't sure. But he was sure he could function well enough and he went over his plan again and thought it should work.

So after breakfast, with the sun shining again, he drove his car to the gate where he'd been the day before and parked it. There was plenty of space with evidence of buildings having been removed and bits and pieces of junk lying around. He found an empty, old metal dustbin which he thought should serve his purpose well. There didn't seem to be anybody around for miles and he started banging on this with another big piece of metal he found. It made a very loud noise which was exactly his intention as he wanted to attract the attention of anybody in the forest. He took frequent breaks, first to give his arm a rest as it was quite hard work and secondly to give anybody there the chance to respond.

Then, after about half an hour of doing this, he heard a deep, growly voice from within the forest say, 'What's with all the noise? It's hurting our ears.'

'Sorry about that but I didn't know how else to get your attention. I'd like to talk to your leader if I may.'

'No, you can't. Go away.'

'I'm not going anywhere and I'll make plenty more noise until I get to speak to him.'

'What's your name?'

'Damien. What's yours?'

'Never mind about that. Wait there.'

'I told you I'm not going anywhere.' And with those last few words there was silence again in the forest. Damien waited about half an hour longer, sitting in his car with the windows open so he could hear if there was any response to his request. And finally there was. He heard another voice, also deep and growly but with a slightly more sophisticated accent, say, 'I understand you want to talk to me. I'm the leader of this tribe and my name's Titan. So talk, young man.'

'Can I see you, please?'

'No, I'm afraid not. Now tell me what you want.'

'To do that, I'll have to give you a bit of the background first.' And he went on to explain that he was a journalist from one of the capital's biggest newspapers and how he had come across a document which had recently been declassified. He told his unseen listener that this document seemed to be a contract between the government and some 'indigenous inhabitants' of this forest giving them the land forever and how he wanted to write a story about them. Then he stopped and just waited for a response.

He heard what sounded like a curse but it was in a language he didn't recognise and then the mysterious voice said, 'How did you know there was anybody living here still?'

'Oh, I just looked you up on a website and there was a video of what looked like a village set in the centre of the forest with a number of round dwellings. Unfortunately, however, it was taken at night using infra-red camera technology and there weren't any people around. But I still thought it was worth checking out.'

'I didn't understand all of what you said but I got the gist of it. However, I'd still like you to go away.'

'If I go away, I'll write something but it'll have to be mostly invented, not true, and I'm sure many of our readers will be fascinated by it. You'll probably be plagued by thousands of people coming to see what they can and even perhaps breaking through your fence but if you let me in, I promise to keep your location secret. All I want to do is to see how you survive and live in the forest.' Damien had shot his final bolt now and waited with bated breath for a response.

'You really are a persistent young man, aren't you? We'll see but I have to consult with others first. If you come back tomorrow morning at about 10 am, I should be able to give you a definitive response.'

'Thank you very much for considering my request and yes, I'll be here then. Can I ask you a question now?'

'Yes, I suppose so although I don't promise to answer it.'

'Are you leprechauns?' There! He'd asked the most important question of all!

'Whatever makes you ask that? Anyway, if we decide to let you in, you'll get your answer tomorrow morning.'

'OK. Please don't forget that I'm on your side.' Then he heard a kind of harrumph from the voice and that was the end of the conversation. So he got back into his car and decided to go back to the pub where his trusty laptop was waiting for him. He was elated by the turn of events, however, realising that the tribe's leader had all but confirmed his suspicions. But, before he left, he tried using his mobile phone to ring Luella. However, to his great surprise, there didn't seem to be any kind of signal available there.

When he got back, he had lunch and then went up to his room and continued typing up his notes. Then he reread them all and decided there were nearly enough already for the book which he was still hoping to write about his experiences there. After that he wondered what he could do with the rest of the day and thought he might go out for a proper walk as he'd told the landlady was his intention all along.

So he went downstairs and asked his landlady if it was possible to walk to the sea from the pub and she told him a shortcut but said it would be pretty muddy. He wasn't afraid of that and set off at a brisk pace, finally arriving at the coast where he was confronted by the wild Atlantic Ocean. From there he walked along a path some little way before returning to the pub. He was hungry again and had dinner with a few of the oldies but refrained from mentioning the possibility of there being leprechauns in the forest. Then he was tired and went upstairs, called his wife mainly to ask about their baby, and, after a shower, just went to bed, well-satisfied with his day.

Chapter

7

That's enough about Damien for the moment. Let's turn now to the fairies. It was said at the beginning of this account that not much had happened in the past ten years. This was true as far as their relations with humans had gone. However, something important *had* happened which will have a bearing on this story. If you remember, nearly at the end of *This Forest is Ours*, the fairies threw a big party to celebrate their victory in getting their contract with the humans, and they invited the leprechauns to it. Both Gwendolyn, the queen of the fairies, and Titan, the king of the leprechauns, hoped this would forge links between especially the children of the two species and they were successful in doing this, perhaps too successful according to the elderly members of each tribe. This was because two of the older teenagers became powerfully attracted to each other, the girl a fairy and the boy a leprechaun.

When these two turned twenty, they asked permission of their parents to get married as they were now, according to custom, adults. This threw both tribes into an uproar, dividing them almost equally according to age, the elderly members being against it as they were more traditional and the younger ones saying, 'If they're in love, we can't stop them.' Titan and Gwendolyn ended up having to arbitrate and they decided in favour of them but they both had to sign a contract, saying that, **if** they had any living children, and it was a big if as this had never been tried before, they would have to bring them up for six months with the leprechauns and six months with the fairies each year. This way the children would hopefully get the best education of both tribes. This was a clever compromise and, although there were still a very few who thought the whole idea was mad, most of both the tribes agreed with it, and Gwendolyn and Titan were praised for their wisdom.

So they got married and a year later the girl had a miscarriage early on in her pregnancy. But they didn't give up trying to have a baby and, after another miscarriage the following year, the year after that she finally carried the baby to term. It was, however, a difficult birth as the baby was bigger than a normal fairy one and she ended up with the surgeons being forced to give her a Caesarean. This was very unusual for them to have to do but, fortunately, it went well and the baby, a boy, was born healthy with the little wing nubs of fairy babies and the slightly webbed feet of the leprechauns, and the mother survived.

Fairies always tended to heal quickly and true to form, she was soon weaning the baby off breast milk and onto solids. The baby was at this time living with the fairies and everybody was very interested in it, often coming to visit the mother and father so they could look at it. It was open house also for the leprechauns who came too.

Then, because it was clearly going to survive, it was time to name the baby – this was both a fairy and a leprechaun custom and it provoked the first argument between the mother and the father, the mother wanting a fairy name and the father a leprechaun one. When they couldn't agree, they took the problem to Gwendolyn who decided, after a few days' thought and a consultation with Titan, that perhaps they could call the boy by an old Irish name, used by humans.

This was because she was thinking of the future where the boy might have to integrate into human society and both parents agreed with this. So they decided to call him Owen, which in ancient times was spelt Eoin and was a name also used by the leprechauns, and everybody was happy at last.

Owen grew up tall (for a leprechaun!) and strong but, being forced to live with the fairies for half of every year, he was also very gentle and kind with the fairy children, even if he was very mischievous and often the despair of his parents. For example, he was utterly fearless and would climb the highest trees he could find right to the very top if that was possible. But everybody loved him and, in return, he loved everybody back. His wings also grew at a great rate and, by the time this story takes place, he could flutter them successfully although he still couldn't fly. He was seven when Damien turned up on the scene and a very quick learner but of course he was still a child.

And what of Gwendolyn at this time? Of course she was ten years older and wiser than she had been when she went on her first big adventure to the capital with Titan. This had seemingly cured her of her desire to find out more about the humans and she told her husband, Finn, that she seriously hoped she would have no more to do with them, much to his relief. So she settled back into her old routine of looking after the castle and was apparently happy doing that. She was lucky also in still having her old friend, Roisin, as her High Priestess and advisor, and often turned to her when she needed help with something.

So that was, very briefly, a summary of the situation in the fairy castle adjoining the forest where the leprechauns lived and everything looked set fair for the future until Damien arrived.

Chapter 8

Titan at once called his Council together and asked them for advice on what he should do about this troublesome human, stressing the need for caution and relaying Damien's words as precisely as he could remember. The Council was split almost exactly down the middle, with half of them arguing that they shouldn't give in to threats and should just tell him to go away in the strongest possible terms, while the other half said that since the contract was now out in the open, what harm could it do to let him in and see how they lived? They added a few sensible provisos though. Titan thought about their arguments and then decided that he needed to visit Gwendolyn in her castle to ask for her advice and this was an idea they could all agree with.

So he strode off through the forest towards the sea, keeping to the hidden leprechaun paths, until he came to the small fields beyond, where the fairies grew their vegetables, flowers and herbs for eating. Then it was up the flight of big stairs to the main gate of the castle which he rapped on hard. A guard immediately opened it and said, recognising him, 'What can we do for you, My Lord?'

'I need to speak to your queen on a matter of some urgency,' Titan said.

'Do come in,' the guard said politely and he entered the main castle. 'I think she's in her private quarters,' the guard said now and Titan replied, 'Don't worry. I know where they are,' and he proceeded there on his own. When he got there, he tapped on the door which opened quickly and he was confronted by Finn, the queen's husband.

'To what do we owe this honour?' Finn asked.

'I have to speak to Her Majesty. It's important,' Titan said brusquely.

'Well, come in, old chap. She's here.' And Titan followed him into the private quarters and down the passage into their small, cosy sitting room where Gwendolyn was reading. She was looking fine, he noticed, with her blonde hair loose although, when he looked hard at her, he could see a few grey hairs starting to appear and he thought to himself, well, none of us are getting any younger. His own hair had turned white a few years ago although it was still thick and he didn't feel old.

She jumped up when he came in and said, 'Titan! How good to see you!'

'Thank you, My Lady, but I'm afraid I'm the bearer of bad news.' And he went on to tell her in a few succinct sentences, which he'd been rehearsing in his head on the way there, how the contract had been released into the wider world and how it had been seen by Damien, a reporter for a Dublin newspaper, how he'd talked to him and what he'd said. 'And now I'm not sure what to do,' he said morosely.

The queen, who'd been listening to all this intently but not interrupting the flow of words, said now with a serious look on her face, 'Yes, that is indeed very bad news. But we will try to find a solution. And, whatever happens, you can be assured of our help.'

'Thank you for that. My Council is equally split over what we should do, half of them saying we should send him away with a flea in his ear and the other half in favour of letting him in with a few provisos, such as insisting that we had the ultimate right to refuse to let him publish what he writes and that he should show us what he's written before it goes to his boss.'

'I'm not surprised. It's a difficult problem. And, as I said, we will certainly help if we can, especially since it might affect us in the longer term. But wait a minute! I've just had an idea! Obviously the ones on your Council who are against letting him in are worried about his intentions and whether he can be trusted. Maybe I can help with that. Do you remember the special power I had to read the humans' minds?' When Titan nodded and said 'Of course I do', she continued, 'Well, I've still got them and would be prepared to use them on your troublesome reporter. They're probably a bit rusty by now after all this time but I don't see why I shouldn't be able to find out whether you can trust him. What do you think?'

'Yes! I think that's a brilliant idea! It'd be like it was when you signalled to me if the drivers of our transport to the capital could be trusted all those years ago!'

'Yes, exactly. Maybe I could meet him in disguise and scan his brain.'

Now Titan was all fired up and he said, 'We're meeting him tomorrow morning at 10 am at the gate for our decision. Would that be too soon for you?'

'No, I don't see why it should be. If I come to your camp at, say, 9.30 wearing my camouflage uniform and the shawl you gave me over my hair, do you think that would be OK?'

'It sounds perfect to me. Don't forget to tape up your wings really well.'

'I won't. OK, I'll meet you then.' So that was decided.

Finn, meanwhile, had been listening to all this without saying a word but now he interrupted, saying, 'Yes, I agree with my wife. This is probably the quickest and easiest way to find out his intentions.'

'Thank you, darling, and now I'm sure you need to get back to your Council, Titan, and tell them what we've decided.'

'I do indeed and thank you very much, Your Majesty.' And with those final words he left.

Gwendolyn knew that the first thing she needed to do now was to check where her camouflage uniform was and it was, indeed, in the same chest where she'd put it all that time ago. She also found some tape to tape up her wings with and the shawl to put over her hair. That done, she felt she was ready so she just carried on with her day as normal. To tell the truth, she was excited about being able to use her unusual power for a legitimate purpose after all this time.

Chapter

9

Gwendolyn didn't sleep very well that night, thinking about what the next day might bring and what the implications of failure might mean to both the fairies and the leprechauns, and neither did Damien, who was worried about whether the whole journey had been wasted. But he got up quite early, had a decent breakfast, noticed that the weather was set fair and then read the paper until it was time to leave. He had decided to leave his mobile phone at the pub: first, because of the obvious lack of signal in the forest and second, in case he was tempted to take any photos of the leprechauns, which he suspected wouldn't go down very well with them.

He left his rented car in the same place as the day before, getting there about 10 minutes before the scheduled time. Meanwhile Gwendolyn and Titan had already arrived as they wanted to be early to find a good place for Gwendolyn to hide in the undergrowth where she would be able to see Damien clearly. They didn't want him to see her at all unless it was unavoidable. Several of Titan's trusted lieutenants were also present, including the man who had met Damien first, and Gwendolyn had briefed them all about possible scenarios and the signal she would give Titan if Damien passed the test and also the one if he didn't.

So everyone was in place when Titan called out to Damien, who was standing right next to the gate, which suited Gwendolyn. She eyed him up and down from her hiding place and decided at once she liked what she saw but she knew from personal experience how deceptive appearances could be, especially with humans.

He replied at once, 'Yes, I'm here!'

Titan said now, 'We just want to put you through a little test to find out how trustworthy you are. It's nothing to worry about, just relax as much as possible.'

Damien said suspiciously, 'What kind of test?'

This response threw Titan for a moment but then he said, quite truthfully, 'We have someone with us who has the ability to read your mind. So, as I said, just relax.'

'Oh, is that all?' Damien said sarcastically.

'Do you want to come in or not?'

'Yes, very much.'

'Then I'm sorry but this is a condition of ours. And there is one other condition also: you must absolutely guarantee that you will let us vet anything you write before you publish it in your newspaper.'

'As to your second condition, yes, I will guarantee that I will let you vet anything I write before publication. I always do that anyway with all my interviewees. And as to the first, OK, go ahead and test me. I don't think I've got anything to hide anyway.'

'That's good. So you're prepared to cooperate?'

'Yes.'

'Good. Now relax as much as possible.'

Damien tried to empty his mind but this was difficult to do and then he remembered some meditation he'd done a long time ago when he was at university and focussed on an empty stretch of beach with a blue sea glittering just behind. Suddenly he felt eyes on him and a peculiar tingling which seemed to come directly from his mind. Then, almost immediately, he appeared to go into some kind of trance state and found his innermost thoughts being revealed, although as he'd just said to Titan, there was nothing he was particularly ashamed of. In spite of the fact that he had no idea how long the whole thing lasted, it wasn't particularly uncomfortable, just very strange.

When he came out of the state, he looked around, completely bewildered, and suddenly noticed what seemed to be a small woman disappearing into the forest.

Then he called out, 'That was probably the strangest thing that ever happened to me. Was it witchcraft?'

'Of a sort,' he heard Titan call back. 'But the important thing for you is that you passed the test. We are going to open the gate now.'

He rubbed his slightly sore head, wonderingly, and said, 'Really?'

'Yes, you appear to be an honest sort of human. So now you can see us.'

Then Damien was confronted by the most astonishing sight: A group of very small men, all clearly barefoot, emerged from the bushes. They all seemed to be wearing rags and tatters and had massive chests with long, unkempt black beards and were all carrying a menacing array of weapons, including shields, spears and swords, but there was not a gun to be seen. They looked like bandits from the tenth century to Damien or, perhaps more accurately, like the hobbits he had seen in the films of Tolkien's *Lord of the rings* plus weapons. He stared at them for a couple of seconds in awe and then said without thinking, 'So you really *are* leprechauns!'

'Yes, indeed and proud of it,' Titan said. He was clearly their leader, Damien knew, not least because he was wearing a gold crown and had a mane of thick, white hair, making him look older than the others.

'Very pleased to meet you gentlemen,' Damien said politely, knowing instinctively that he had to be careful when talking to these 'people' as probably they didn't understand modern English with all its slang. One of the men was busy opening the gate and as soon as it was open Damien slipped through and shook Titan's hand vigorously. He was surprised by the strength of the leprechaun's grip and decided that, just because they were small, he couldn't afford to underestimate their strength or their determination to retain their privacy.

Then Titan said, 'Follow me but be careful to tread exactly in my footprints. We wouldn't want a guest to go astray and fall foul of one of the many human traps we have put around here.'

Damien blanched when he heard this but just replied, 'OK.' And they all set off in a long line with Titan leading and Damien following directly behind him with his eyes on the ground. He felt for the strap of his laptop in its waterproof case under his jacket and then for his notebook and pen in an inner pocket and found everything was where it should be. Then he thought of the million and one questions he wanted to ask Titan when they got to his camp. He was also trying to remember everything he had learnt when he was young about leprechauns but, unfortunately, he could actually remember very few details. Well, I'm soon going to find out, he thought. So the 20-minute-or-so walk passed very quickly for him.

Chapter 10

When he got to the camp in the big clearing in the forest, Damien recognised it from the infra-red pictures he had seen but it appeared quite a bit larger in reality. There were a lot of the little, round houses seemingly sunk into the ground as they were so low, made of some kind of vegetation which he couldn't identify. There were also quite a few children running around and he saw his first leprechaun women who all appeared to be doing normal things like hanging clothes out to dry. It looked to Damien like a traveller encampment but he didn't have time to admire the scene as many of the smaller children came running over towards him. They asked him what he was in broken English and he told them that he was a human. This seemed to fascinate them but they were quickly shooed away by their mothers and Titan who told them he was a guest and didn't want to be disturbed just yet.

Then he led Damien up to one of the biggest dwellings which he entered, beckoning to him to follow, and he had to bend a little so as not to hit his head on the ceiling. Titan at once called out a name which sounded to Damien like Dronfeld. A squat little lady came out from behind a kind of curtain which seemed to be made of animal furs and Titan introduced her as his wife. Damien immediately went up to her and held out his hand, saying, 'How do you do, ma'am?' but she ignored it and simply bowed to him. So he took his hand back quickly and bowed to her instead. Titan said now, approvingly, 'You're a quick learner. Our ladies don't like being touched by strangers, not even other leprechauns, unless they're children of course, only by other members of the family,' and Damien replied 'I'll certainly remember that.' 'Can you get us some tea please, dear?' Titan asked his wife and she disappeared without a word.

Now Titan said, 'Come and sit down, Damien,' indicating a nearby chair, and Damien was very pleased to do this, even though the chair was very low like in a primary school classroom, as he was afraid of getting a permanent crick in his neck from the low ceiling. Damien now had a chance to look around him, which he took eagerly, noticing the many candles which lit up the scene and made it feel very homely. 'So tell me, what are your first impressions of how we live?' Titan asked now after he'd given Damien a few moments to collect his thoughts.

'Well, my first impression is how lovely and warm your houses are.'

'Yes, they are, aren't they? That's because they are made entirely of peat which is an excellent insulator and we also have a brazier going full-time, fuelled also by peat which burns slowly and evenly.'

'That's amazing! I have so many questions to ask you.'

'It's not amazing. We have plenty of peat bogs in the forest which are continually being replenished. We have used peat as our primary building material and fuel for centuries.'

'I stand corrected. Can I ask you a question now?'

'Yes. Go ahead.'

'What do you eat?'

'Oh, mainly rabbits and voles and other small animals we find in the forest along with nuts and berries which we harvest when they're in season. Occasionally we go on hunts for bigger animals, deer especially, even wolves sometimes. And we keep goats for their meat and their milk.'

'So you're primarily meat eaters, are you?' Damien meanwhile was taking shorthand notes of everything he was being told in his notebook.

'Yes, that's right. And we're pretty healthy. It's rare to find one of us sick.' But now he was interrupted by his wife who came in bringing a couple of rough, earthenware mugs which were giving off the most interesting aroma. She handed one to her husband and one to Damien. He took a cautious sip and said, 'This is lovely. What's in it?'

'Just some forest herbs, that's all,' Titan said.

'Well, I like it. I'd like to know more about the herbs you use. Presumably you use them for medicines too?'

'Yes. You're absolutely right. I'll have to introduce you to our doctor.'

'That would be fantastic,' Damien said, thinking that, although he enjoyed talking to Titan, the more ordinary members of the tribe he could meet, the better.

'Now you must excuse me. I'm afraid I have to go on a hunt now. But you may talk to any of my tribe who aren't going. I know that the children are dying to meet you and I will tell our doctor that you are available now and that you would like to meet her. I hope you can stay for dinner as we're having a bit of a feast tonight.'

'Thank you very much indeed, Titan, for all your kindness but I'll have to call my wife and my boss this evening. I hope the dinner is not in my honour.'

'No, certainly not. We had it scheduled already. It's one of our annual festivals. But that's ok. I did spring it on you rather abruptly. Maybe you could come and have our evening meal with us tomorrow? I could meet you at 10 am in the morning again if you wished as I'm sure you will still have many questions for us.'

'Yes, you're absolutely right about that. I would be delighted to meet you again tomorrow morning. As for the evening, let's see, shall we? I may be too tired.'

'Yes, that's fine. I'll get someone to escort you back to the gate.'

'Thank you once again for everything, Titan.'

'That's all right. If you get hungry, just tell my wife. Goodbye then and see you tomorrow morning.' And with those parting words he collected a fearsome-looking spear from behind one of the curtains and left.

Damien sat back in his little chair, stretched out his legs and relaxed for a few minutes, thinking about all the things he'd learnt already and just drinking in the atmosphere in the hut. When he'd first entered, he was struck by the strange smell inside but he didn't mention it for fear of offending Titan. However, it wasn't at all a bad smell, just earthy and primitive, and now he realised it must be the normal smell of the leprechauns. He was truly amazed by the hospitality he'd received until he realised, perhaps rather cynically, that Titan was probably trying to prove to him how basically civilised his tribe was and how much they deserved to live their own style of life. And he was rapidly coming to the conclusion that they were right. He now wasn't at all sure that he would actually publish his findings but he was still determined to find out as much about their society as he possibly could.

As all these thoughts were going through his mind, he decided to type up his notes from this morning on his laptop so that at least he would have a proper record of them. So he took off his jacket, rolled up his long T-shirt sleeves, took his laptop out of its case and started typing. But he hadn't got very far when suddenly he felt a draught at his back and he turned around. And there in the doorway stood a motley group of children. He thought they looked like some of the beggar children he'd seen sometimes on the streets of the capital. So he closed his laptop and said, 'Do come in, children,' as if this was his own hut.

They hesitated a moment, perhaps wanting to see if Titan's wife was around and would shoo them out, but then seeing that she wasn't, they all came running in and started bombarding Damien with questions. 'What's your name?' 'Are you a human?' 'Where are you from?' all of which Damien answered truthfully while they looked at him goggle-eyed. They were all boys, Damien noticed, not a girl in sight. Then one of the bolder boys saw his laptop and said, 'What's that?'

'In my society it's called a laptop.'

'What does it do?' he asked now, coming up to it and picking it up.

'It does lots of things but I mainly use it for typing up my notes after I've spoken to somebody. That's what I was doing when you came in. But be careful with it. It's a bit fragile.'

The boy looked rather disappointed with this reply but asked a good question now, after putting it carefully back down on the table in front of Damien. 'Does it play any games?'

'Yes, indeed it does. Would you like to see one of them?'

'Yes, please!' they all chorused.

Damien didn't often play games on his computer but there were a couple he did play when he was bored. He opened it up and switched it over to games and then to one of them, a sci-fi thriller game which he liked and which he thought the children might enjoy. Quickly he was in the business of battling bad aliens and destroying evil alien spacecraft. The children were totally silent while he was playing, obviously fascinated by the game and the sounds it made. But after a few minutes Damien stopped and said, 'I think that's enough now. Would you like to have a go?' So Damien set it up for 4 players and the children were soon trying it out happily with Damien giving instructions. They were quick learners and, in spite of their fat little fingers, were soon playing happily with some of the others watching.

Then, for the first time, Damien had the chance to look up at the audience and he suddenly noticed one boy who was a bit taller than the others watching avidly but there was one very strange thing about him. He had wings!

Chapter 11

Do you remember the half-fairy, half-leprechaun boy who was mentioned earlier in this account? Now he comes into his own and adds a whole new perspective on what Damien has found out so far.

He beckoned to the boy, who came up to him, and said, 'What's your name, boy?'

'Owen, if it pleases you,' he replied very politely and clearly. 'What's yours?'

'Damien. Why are you wearing wings, Owen?'

'I'm not wearing them! They're always here!'

'And why is that if I may ask?'

'Because I'm half fairy and half leprechaun. My mother's fairy and my father's leprechaun.'

Damien took a few moments to process this astonishing information, then asked, 'Is your mother around?'

'Yes, she should be. I live half the year with the fairies and half with the leprechauns. At the moment I'm living with the leprechauns.'

'Can I meet her, do you think?'

'Yes, I don't see why not. When? Right now?'

'That would be great! Thanks very much, Owen.'

'Anything to help an honoured guest of Titan's.'

'Just one moment, please,' and Damien turned back to the other boys who were all still avidly playing his game and not paying any attention to this conversation. 'If I leave you alone for a little while, do you think you'll be able to look after my computer. Remember it's very valuable to me. If you finish before I come back, just close the lid, OK?'

'Yes, sir,' said one of the older boys. 'We'll look after it for you.'

'Thank you,' Damien said. Then he got up from his chair and followed Owen outside. He asked him while they were walking, 'Where do you live when you're with the fairies?'

'Oh, they have a big castle by the sea through the forest over there,' he said, gesticulating.

Now Damien was getting really excited, thinking, 'Could this be true?' Then he asked another question, 'How old are you, Owen?'

'I'm seven,' he said proudly. 'I should soon be able to fly.' And he fluttered his wings to show what he could do with them.

'That's fantastic!' Damien said perfectly truthfully.

But then they came up to one of the typical smaller huts and Owen ran inside, shouting for his mother, saying, 'I've brought someone to meet you.' Damien waited outside and very quickly Owen came back out, followed by what was clearly a woman fairy, a little taller than any of the leprechauns he'd met yet, with long blond hair, bright blue-green eyes and the most lustrous white wings imaginable. She was heavily pregnant, he noticed.

Damien was totally stunned by this vision and at a loss for words which was very unusual for him. She eyed him up and down and then said, 'You're clearly the human Titan invited into the camp but I didn't expect to meet you.'

Her words took Damien out of his trance and he went up to her and held out his hand but them remembered his manners and bowed instead. 'I am indeed. My name's Damien and I certainly didn't expect to meet a real fairy here.'

'Well, now you have. What can I do for you?'

'Do you think it might be possible for me to visit your castle by the sea which Owen has told me about?'

She bit her lip then and said, 'Owen been talking out of turn again, has he? Well, I'm not at all sure. I'd have to ask my queen.'

'Would you mind doing that? I'll be back again tomorrow morning,' Damien asked, putting on his most pleading expression with his biggest puppy-dog eyes which he knew usually worked with human ladies.

She looked at him closely and then said, 'I heard that my queen vouched for you already, so all right. Today is actually quite a good time for me as my husband is out on a big hunt at the moment and I don't have anything particularly important to do until he gets back later. I'll give you your answer tomorrow morning.'

'Thank you so much. I'm extremely grateful. I also have lots of questions for you so even if I'm not invited to your castle, can I come back tomorrow and ask a few of them?'

'Yes, I don't see why not provided that I can ask you a few of my own.'

'Of course you can. Well, I'll leave you now and see you tomorrow,' Damien said in parting and he turned and went back to Titan's hut, feeling elated with what he'd discovered – something completely unexpected - where he found his computer with the lid closed and no sign of the boys. But he left Owen with his mother who said she wanted to talk to him. He hoped he hadn't got the child in trouble.

Then he realised Titan's wife was bustling around somewhere and that must be why the boys had left. His stomach was rumbling now, always a sign that he was hungry, and he remembered Titan saying to him that if he wanted food, he could just ask her. So he called out to her and asked her if he could have something to eat. She disappeared without a word but reappeared very soon with a dish of cold meat and berries. He wolfed it all down as it was delicious and then sat back full, wondering what the most useful thing he could do now was. He thanked her very much for the lovely meal when she came in to clear everything away and then looked at his watch but he still had a couple of hours before he had to go back. He didn't fancy going back to his typing after what he'd just discovered.

But then the problem was solved for him when there was a tentative knock on the door. He said, 'Come in,' and a female leprechaun put her head round it and said, 'I'm the doctor around here. Titan told me you'd be interested to speak to me.'

'Yes, indeed. Thank you very much for coming,' Damien said, getting up and bowing.

'I was here earlier but I noticed a big group of boys in here and decided to come back later.'

'I'm sorry I wasn't here. I had something important to do.' Damien was sure he must have blushed when he said this as 'something important' must be the understatement of the year. 'Do sit down.'

She sat and Damien tried to remember the questions he wanted to ask her but his mind was completely blank, full only of the revelation he'd just been presented with. However, they did return and he asked her first, 'Where did you train if I may ask?'

'Here under my predecessor. Our knowledge is passed down orally from generation to generation.'

'OK. That makes perfect sense. And I presume that all the medications you prescribe are based on plants you find in the forest?'

'Yes, most of them. A few come from animals – for example, I find that rabbit's liver is good for indigestion if it's well cooked.'

'Really? That's interesting. I'm sure you could have a lot to teach us humans,' Damien said, furiously scribbling in his notebook.

'I'm sure I could although I think you could probably teach us more. For example, I've heard that you use something you call antibiotics. I'd like to know more about them. But I don't see that happening, do you? We're pretty cut off here.'

'No, I agree. But you seem to do a pretty good job with what you've got. All the people here seem very healthy to me.'

'Yes, that's true. My talents are not often called upon. It's mainly injuries caused for men by hunting. Wolves especially can be very dangerous. The women all seem to be immune to disease so I only very rarely have to treat them, except occasionally in childbirth.'

'So it's probably better for you that you are cut off, no?'

She considered this idea for a few seconds and then said slowly, 'Yes, I think you are probably right.'

'What about when the leprechauns get very old?'

'They usually just pass away peacefully in bed.'

'Lucky you! Humans are prone to so many incurable diseases when they get old.'

'That's interesting.'

'Unfortunately I'm not a doctor so I can't really teach you anything about our medical practices but I do have a few more questions for you.'

'Ask away.'

'Were you present when Owen was born?'

'Yes, I was,' she replied, looking rather uncomfortable at the question.

'And where did that happen?' Damien pressed.

'Oh, not far away,' she said and refused to say any more on the topic, probably having been told by Titan not to reveal the presence of the fairies, Damien thought.

'OK. I didn't mean to pry,' Damien said. 'Just two more questions, I think. What is the most useful forest plant for you?'

She looked much happier now they were off the subject of Owen and answered readily, 'It's probably a type of forest moss which grows on the trees around here and is very useful for treating hunting wounds.'

'One final question: Do the leprechauns keep any pets? The reason I ask is twofold. First because I haven't seen any around and secondly because I was wondering if you had sometimes to treat animals like our vets do.'

'Interesting questions. And the simple answer is no to your first question, probably because cats and dogs never stray into the forest and so our people hardly even know what they look like. However, that said, Titan used to have a huge dog as a working pet but he died about two years ago of old age and he was very cut up about it, even insisting that we had a public funeral for it and proclaiming a day's mourning. So don't, whatever you do, mention pets to him.'

'Ok. I won't. Do you, by any chance, know what breed it was?'

'I think you call them Irish wolfhounds. And, as to your second question, the answer is occasionally I do have to treat animals, usually our goats when they get sick and the occasional bird with a broken wing, brought to me by the children. But it's all pretty simple stuff.'

'OK. Thank you very much for talking to me. I found it fascinating,' and with that Damien finished his notes, got up and bowed to her again.

She too got up then and bowed back saying, 'No, thank you. I too found it interesting. You are the first human I've ever spoken to.'

'Well, I hope I haven't made too bad an impression on you.'

'No, not at all. You're not nearly as scary as I've been led to believe all humans are.'

This remark made him smile and she smiled back. Then she took her leave. Damien looked at his watch and thought it was probably time to go back to the pub now. So he called Titan's wife who was just outside sitting in the warm sunshine and asked her if she could find the man who had been deputed by her husband to take him back through the forest. She arrived back with him just as he had finished packing everything away and, after saying goodbye to Titan's wife and thanking her again for the lovely lunch and for all her help, he left following the leprechaun.

He got back safely to the pub and went straight up to his room where he had a quick shower and then, after changing his clothes, went downstairs where he had an early dinner. After that he went back up to his room again to phone his wife whom he asked about the baby and her work that day and managed to escape from without giving any news of his own. Then he rang his boss. He told Luella a little about his day with the leprechauns but not mentioning the fairies as, superstitiously, he didn't want to pre-empt the issue, fearing that it might all go wrong the next day. She cried out with delight, 'I knew you'd come up trumps! Well done, Damien!'

to which he replied, 'Please remember to keep this all under your hat until you see what I have written.' This made her serious again and she answered, 'Yes, of course I will. I know how important that is,' before ringing off.

Then he got out his trusty computer and typed up his notes of the day which took him the rest of the evening after which he just sank into bed and fell asleep almost immediately, tired after his long and dramatic day.

Chapter 12

Damien woke up quite early, feeling rested but excited by what might happen that day. He looked out of the window and saw that it was drizzling slightly but this didn't bother him as long as it wasn't a full-on storm. After washing he went downstairs and had breakfast before reading the papers, which reminded him of something he wanted to ask the leprechauns and he made a note of it in his notebook, until it was time to go. He decided not to take his laptop with him that day as he didn't want to be encumbered by it, especially if he was to actually meet some fairies, relying only on his trusty notebook and pen. He also decided not to take his mobile phone, for the same reasons as yesterday. Anyway, he reckoned there wouldn't be much chance to use it.

He drove over to the gate to the forest and leaving the car to one side in its usual place he walked up to it and called out, 'Is anyone there?' An answer came back very quickly, 'Yes.' And a leprechaun came and opened the gate for him. He went through it and followed the leprechaun carefully but without talking back to the camp. There he thanked him and went over to Titan's hut. But he didn't seem to be there so he went to see if he could find Owen's mother, which was even more important, he felt, than speaking to Titan. The whole camp seemed very quiet and he thought that perhaps everyone was still sleeping off the excesses of the night before.

But she was there outside hanging up some laundry although there was no sign of Owen. He went up to her and bowed. 'Hello again,' she said before continuing in her funny, sing-song way of pronouncing English which he was rapidly getting used to, 'I know why you are here. And the answer is yes, you can go to the castle. The fairies took quite a bit of persuading but they realised in the end that, having seen me and Owen who had told you anyway about the castle, they might as well invite you. You were lucky that it was the queen herself who vouched for you. You will have to walk with me there though. I will be your passport inside.' Or words to that effect.

'Thank you very much indeed for doing that. I'm exceedingly grateful,' Damien said, 'and of course I'd be happy to walk with you. When should we leave?'

'I think in about half an hour. I have a few chores I have to do first.'

'That's fine by me. I still haven't seen Titan yet this morning.'

'I told him last night about your coming to the castle today and he was surprised that they had invited you. But when I explained the circumstances, he understood.'

'OK. Well, thank you for doing that. It certainly saves me having to explain. So I'll see you in half an hour. Oh, and I do hope I didn't get Owen into trouble yesterday.'

'Fine. And no, you didn't. I'm used to his behaviour.'

'Good. Well, that's a relief.' And he bowed again and left her, heading back towards Titan's hut and checking his watch. He noticed it had even stopped drizzling and the sun was starting to shine. Even the weather's smiling on me, he thought to himself. I am truly a lucky guy.

When he got there, he found Titan outside yawning and stretching prodigiously but he greeted Damien with no signs of tiredness. 'Good day to you, young man,' he said. 'You caught me doing my morning exercises.'

'And to you, Titan,' Damien replied. 'How did the party go?'

'It went well, thanks. Most of the tribe is still sleeping it off. Would you like to come inside and have some tea? I'm just about to have some.'

'Yes, I'd love some,' Damien replied and followed him inside where Dronfeld was already waiting with a cup for Titan who asked her to bring another cup for their guest which she quickly did. They sat down and drank their tea contentedly and then Titan said, 'If you have any more questions for me, now might be a good time to ask. I understand you're off to visit the fairies this morning and I think you'll probably have even more questions to ask them.'

'That may be true. First, I'd like to ask you whether your people can read and write.' This was the question he'd written in his notebook before he left that morning.

'Do you mean English?'

'No, not only. In any language.'

'Well,' he answered slowly, 'only a very few of us can read some English although it's mainly for what we need, like street signs in the city, and none of us has really learnt to write it. We don't need it, you see. We're quite happy without books. But many of us can understand it when spoken and can reply adequately as you've probably noticed. But, when it comes to our own language, most of us can read and write that. You know that we speak an ancient kind of Elvish, I think you call it in English, which is all we need for communicating. And when it comes to writing it, we use the ancient runes, as do the fairies, by the way. But please don't think we're uneducated savages. We know the ways of the forest much better than you ever could, for example.'

'Of course I don't. That's fascinating. As a journalist, as I'm sure you'll appreciate, I have to rely on a literate population to read what I say. I haven't seen any examples of your runes. I wonder if you could show me some.'

'Yes, sure. But they are not very interesting. Just simple messages which I use for sending to other leprechaun tribes.' Now he got up, went over to his desk and picked up a few pieces of paper before coming back with them and handing them to him. Damien looked at them and saw what resembled, to his inexperienced eyes, a lot of tiny pictograms which looked a bit like Egyptian hieroglyphs.

'Fascinating!' Damien breathed. 'I wish I could learn how to interpret these,' thinking about the other leprechaun tribes he had mentioned.

'You'll have to stay with us much longer than you can to be able to do that,' Titan laughed.

'Yes, I believe you, Titan,' Damien replied. 'To turn now to another issue: I'm interested to know something about the way you govern here.'

'I don't exactly govern all by myself, you know. I have a Council to help me although, if I'm determined on a course of action, I can almost always persuade them to follow me. But, basically, we arbitrate disputes which, fortunately, don't happen very often – we are basically a peace-loving people – and I am responsible for the overall welfare of the tribe. So, if we really need something we can't make for ourselves, for example, I have to depute people to go out and get it for us from the humans.'

'So you use money sometimes? How do you get it?'

'We only use it very occasionally so we have very little here but we get it usually by begging in the streets of the cities. We send out some of the older children, keeping a very careful eye on them, needless to say, and they almost always come up with enough for our needs.'

'Again, fascinating.' Damien looked at his watch now and saw he had to go. 'Thank you for being so open with me. I must leave you now.' And he got up and put his pen back in his inside pocket along with his notebook which was filling up rapidly.

'That's fine. There's not much point in your writing about us if your information doesn't come from the horse's mouth, as it were.'

'That's very true,' said Damien, smiling at the colloquialism. 'Well, I'll see you later, Titan.'

'If the gods are willing,' Titan said in parting, which reminded Damien that he really needed to talk to him about religion, specifically which gods he worshipped. There was still so much he had to learn!

He walked back to the fairy's hut, thinking about everything he'd learned, and found her waiting for him outside, sitting on the grass. There was still no sign of Owen. Also he still hadn't met her husband and asked where he was.

'Oh, he's still in bed. Apparently they had to walk miles before they found a suitable prey, and then he drank a bit too much ale at dinner. So he was tired when he went to bed. Poor darling!'

Damien smiled at this as it reminded him of what his own wife said to her female friends the morning after he came back late from the pub after a few drinks with his colleagues. But there was something more important he wanted to ask. 'Can you fly in your state?' he said, pointing to her stomach which stretched the dress out quite a long way.

'That's a very personal question but yes, I can,' she replied, laughing, 'but not very well, unfortunately. I prefer to walk around at the moment.'

'When are you expecting the baby?'

'Any day now.'

'It's a pity my wife's not here. She's a qualified midwife.'

'Really! That's interesting. It's a pity she wasn't here for Owen's birth. That was difficult. But our own midwives have assured me that the second one should be easier than the first.'

'Good. I hope so.'

By this time they had started walking side by side out of the camp. But they soon came to the forest and the fairy said, 'You must walk exactly behind me now.' So that put paid to any more conversation.

Once again Damien's sense of direction got all messed up and he realised he would definitely need a guide if he was to come this way again. They walked for about twenty minutes and then came out of the forest and Damien gasped. He saw a number of small fields full of flowers and plants of different kinds in front of him which appeared to be very well tended and irrigated by some sort of system which he didn't recognise. But, even more interesting, in front of them was a huge crag with what appeared to be a ruined castle perched on top and with a few small outbuildings next to it. It looked most impressive. He stopped and said, pointing, 'So is that where you live when you're staying with the fairies?'

'Yes, it is,' the fairy said with her tinkly little laugh. 'It doesn't look like much, does it? But wait till you're inside.'

'On the contrary,' Damien said, 'it looks amazing.'

'It's actually much bigger than it looks from here.'

Damien followed her now on a well-trodden path through the fields and side by side they started climbing up a huge flight of steps and over a moat before reaching a massive wooden gate in the wall which she rapped on hard. The gate opened slowly and another fairy with wings appeared who seemed to be male and said, 'Hello. You must be the human. We were told to expect you. Come in.'

His guide then said, 'I will leave you here. I must get back to see to my husband's breakfast.'

'Thank you very much indeed for being my guide,' Damien said.

'That's all right. One of the fairies will bring you back through the forest.' And she turned and left, leaving Damien to wonder how he'd ever managed to get himself in a situation like this.

Then he just followed the guard inside the castle, after being searched for weapons. By the way, you can forget about pictures you might have seen in children's books of fairies as minute little beings sitting on toadstools. They are, in fact, slightly taller than leprechauns, the adults being about the height of an average ten- year-old human child – at least all the fairies Damien was to meet at the castle were.

Chapter 13

When he went in through a second gate, smaller than the first, he was confronted by a large, empty courtyard which was so clean it looked as if you could eat off it. But he didn't have time to dally as his guide was striding ahead of him. 'Where are we going?' he called out.

'To the Council chamber. The queen is waiting for you there.' And that was all he could get out of the swiftly moving guide.

'As long as I'm not about to be thrown in a dungeon,' he muttered to himself. 'Oh well, in for a penny, in for a pound, I guess.' They crossed the courtyard and went through a small door to the left and then up a flight of stairs where his guide (guard?) told him to wait in an empty corridor outside a large door. He rapped on it and was told to come in so he went inside and told someone there that their visitor had arrived. 'Well, show him in,' he heard a silvery, clear voice say. His guide came back outside and said, 'You can go in now.' 'Thank you,' Damien said to his guide but he was already striding off and he wasn't sure if he'd heard.

It was with considerable trepidation that Damien went through the door as he was not at all sure what he'd be confronted with. He saw a large room decorated with a lot of candles with extremely colourful drapes on the walls and baskets of flowers scattered around which were all giving off the most wonderful fragrance. It looked really beautiful and Damien gasped at the sight of it. Then he noticed that there were a number of windows set up high which were letting the morning sunlight in and made it look even more beautiful as the candles didn't need to do so much work. He noticed all this in an instant but then turned his attention to the occupants of the room.

There were nine fairies in it all sitting up on some sort of dais, all women he noted except for one man, and all with the most lovely, soft-looking white wings and all except the man dressed in wonderfully colourful dresses. But then he noticed that they were all scrutinising him with the same amount of interest as he was scrutinising them. None of them had said anything yet.

But then the woman in the middle of the group, who had long blonde hair with a few white streaks in it and blue-green eyes like all the others, said softly, 'Welcome to our castle, Damien. Do sit down. You are probably the first human ever to have been invited in willingly. We understand that you may want to include something about us fairies in what you propose to write about the leprechauns. Is this right?'

'With your kind permission, yes, I would like that very much. And I would like to thank you very much indeed for inviting me. I am greatly honoured.' Then he paused before continuing, 'I feel very stupid in asking this but are you the queen here and, if so, how do I address you?'

The question made her laugh and she said, 'I am indeed. And you may call me Milady like most of the castle does. I think Your Majesty is much too formal, don't you? But let me introduce the rest of my Council.' And she proceeded to go round the table with all their names which he promptly forgot except for one, the male fairy, who she introduced as 'Finn, my husband.'

'I am very pleased to meet you all.' Damien was starting to relax a bit now, knowing that he'd been accepted by this kind lady. 'May I ask you another question now?'

'Yes, why not?' she said.

But now she was interrupted by one of her Council who said, 'Don't we have some business to attend to with Damien before he starts asking his questions?'

'Oh, yes. Of course we do. I completely forgot about it in the excitement of the moment,' the queen said. Then she added, 'I understand you have an arrangement with Titan that he can vet anything you want to print before it comes out. Is this true? And, if so, we hope that you will extend the same courtesy to us.'

Damien remembered now the initial conversation he'd had with Titan where he had indeed promised him such a thing and he nodded, saying vigorously, 'Yes, it's true and of course I will do the same for you. It's something I always do for my interviewees. Although I'm coming to the conclusion that I may not print anything at all about either of your societies, as I'm becoming more and more convinced that you all deserve to be left alone.'

'That may be the wisest move on your part,' the queen said now. 'I do know, however, that you are a very ambitious young man and we all hope that you will stick to your word. We know what a coup it would be if you published an article about us.'

'Have no fear, Milady, my word is my bond. I'm really doing the story now for myself, not my readers.' Then he got a shock as he felt the familiar tingling in his mind and he knew it was being read again. This time, however, it was over much more quickly, in just a few seconds, he reckoned, and there was no residual headache. He looked up at the queen and saw her give a sign to the others in the room. They all seemed to breathe a sigh of relief and she said now, 'I'm sorry about that, Damien, but I'm sure you appreciate we can't be too careful. Anyway, you passed the test again.'

'Thank goodness for that,' Damien said.

'You may ask us whatever you want now.'

He paused a moment to assemble his thoughts before continuing, 'I was wondering what types of plants and vegetables you are growing in the fields I walked through. Presumably you eat most of them?'

One of the council members replied, 'Yes. You're quite right. We eat almost all of them, except the flowers you see around the room which are only for decoration. We are vegetarians, you see.'

'So you're quite different from the leprechauns in that respect,' Damien said now.

'Yes, very.'

'We're also teetotallers. That's another major difference,' the queen added. 'Talking about food, it must be nearly lunchtime,' she said now, looking up at one of the windows above. 'All this talking has made me hungry. Would you like to join us all for lunch, Damien? I'd like to introduce you to the rest of the fairies.'

'Yes, I'd love that,' Damien replied. 'Is there somewhere I can freshen up first?'

'Yes, of course there is. I'll take you to our private quarters,' Finn said. 'It's probably more comfortable there.'

'Thank you very much, Finn. You are all being so kind to me. And, by the way, I love your Council chamber.'

'Thank you for the compliment,' the queen said. 'Most folk find it quite impressive.' Damien filed that remark away for further consideration later and then heard her say to her Councillors, 'We'll meet you all in the main dining room in fifteen minutes,' and with those words she swept out with Damien and Finn following.

They went down the stairs and out into the courtyard where the queen let out an impressive piercing whistle and a guard came running. 'Would you mind tidying up the Council chamber, please?'

'Of course, Milady. Your wish is our command.' And the guard went running off.

Then they continued to another door to the right of the first and went up some more stairs and into the queen's and her husband's private quarters where Finn showed him something he called a 'garderobe', a word Damien wasn't familiar with, but its function was clear and he did what he had to do and washed his hands and face in a basin, drying them on some very soft material and feeling much better afterwards. He realised then that the fairies were really very civilised folk, even if they were out of touch with the modern world, but he knew it was going to take him a very long time to get through all the questions he was bursting to ask. He came out of the bathroom and found Finn outside in what was clearly his study, reading a book.

'What are you reading?' he asked.

'Oh, just some William Shakespeare,' he replied. 'I figured I should brush up on my English if we're going to see more of you.'

'Can I see?' Damien said, trying not to laugh at him for thinking that he spoke Shakespearian English. Finn passed the book over and Damien noticed that it was bound in very fine old leather. Then he looked at the inside cover page and gasped again. It said it had been printed in 1641! 'This book would be worth a small fortune in the human world,' he said.

'We are not interested in money,' Finn said sternly now.

'Oh, I'm so sorry. I didn't mean to annoy you. It was just a natural human reaction to something so valuable.'

'Forgiven and forgotten,' Finn said with a smile. 'I think that's what you say, isn't it?'

'Indeed it is,' Damien replied with an answering smile, relieved that the uncomfortable moment had passed and vowing to himself to watch his language more closely.

'Are you getting hungry?' Finn asked now.

'Yes.' Damien said simply, feeling his stomach rumbling.

'Let me just collect the wife and we'll head down to the big dining room. Are you ready to meet dozens of other fairies?'

'Yes, I……think so,' Damien said hesitantly.

'Don't worry. We don't bite,' Finn said and Damien smiled at his choice of words.

'Your English is really excellent, you know. I don't think there's any need to 'brush it up.'' And Finn smiled broadly at him, clearly pleased with the compliment.

'Come on, wife!' he shouted now in the direction of another closed door. And now the queen appeared, looking radiant, having clearly touched up her makeup and put on yet another beautiful dress, this one made of what looked like red velvet.

'OK. Let's go!' she said and marched out of the room.

'I feel terribly underdressed,' he told her as they crossed the courtyard again, looking down at his muddy boots and creased clothes.

'Don't worry about it. The fairies have no idea what humans usually wear. To them you could be a prince,' she said. These statements reassured Damien a little but not much.

Chapter 14

They came to a very big set of doors which Damien noticed opened with a large, heavy, round wooden latch. He could hear quite a hubbub coming from the room beyond and he wondered how many fairies inhabited the castle but he didn't have time to speculate on this or ask about it as the queen marched straight in with Finn following, and Damien pursuing him rather reluctantly. He went into what was a very large room with high wooden rafters, all beautifully carved, and looked about him.

The hubbub had abruptly ceased on his entry and he was confronted with what looked like hundreds of fairies all sitting at long wooden trestle tables. They were all staring at him and he stared back at them. Then the queen went to the centre of the room and climbed on a chair, presumably so that she could be easily seen by everyone, and said, in her high, very clear voice, 'I would like to introduce a human to you. This is Damien and I have personally invited him here to answer any questions he might have about our way of life. He is a journalist, by the way, but an honourable one, and I hope you will all treat him with respect. I know how unusual it must seem to invite a human here but I judged it to be in our best interests.' No unnecessary words, Damien noticed.

Now she got off the chair and made her way to a kind of raised dais at the end of the room where she sat between all her Councillors with Finn on her right and Damien on her left. He found it rather difficult to sit comfortably he was so much taller than any of the fairies and the chair was very low until he found he could stretch out his legs under the table.

'Now let us pray,' she said. And here she continued in Elvish which Damien understood not a word of. But it was a very short prayer, presumably about giving thanks to their gods for the food they were about to eat, and, as soon as it was over, a number of fairies entered the room from behind him, all dressed in the same kind of uniform, carrying large tureens of soup which gave off the most wonderful aromatic smell. They put the tureens down, one on each table in the room, curtsied to the queen and left. 'Help yourself, Damien,' the queen said now so Damien did, putting the soup in a large wooden bowl in front of him with a long, wooden serving spoon. He took a sip and gasped again for the nth time that day. It was delicious! 'How do you like it?' the queen asked and Damien told her what he thought of it. 'Good! We'll make a fairy of you yet,' she said, grinning. He grinned back at her and proceeded to tuck in avidly.

The soup was surprisingly filling and, when Damien had finished his bowl, he sat back contentedly, and thought about some of the important questions he wanted to ask. He decided to start with religion and asked the queen what gods they worshipped.

'I think it best, if you want to talk about this, to have a word with our High Priestess who knows much more about our religion than anyone else. I'll take you down to meet her after lunch if you wish.'

'Thank you very much. I would be most interested to meet her,' Damien replied.

The main course was a kind of vegetable puree topped with goat's cheese which he also found scrumptious. But lunch, in fact, was soon over and the queen left the room, followed by Damien, with Finn saying he was going back to their private quarters to read. The queen led Damien down a long flight of stone steps into what seemed to be the bowels of the earth where the air was colder than it was up top until she stopped at a door. Damien noticed a sleeping mat outside it and wondered who it was for but then the queen rapped on the door and a head poked round it. A youngish-looking fairy said, 'Who is it?' but, noticing it was the queen herself accompanied by what seemed to be a giant human, she got all flustered and said, 'Oh, it's you Milady. I was just tidying her room a bit. Can you give me a moment?' And she promptly closed the door in their faces.

'Who is she?' Damien asked wonderingly.

'Her name's Ciara. She's the High Priestess' servant. She usually sleeps outside, guarding her door from all comers, although the High Priestess herself is perfectly sociable, I think you'll find. She's also very wise.'

They waited outside for a minute and then Ciara poked her head round the door again and said, 'You can come in now, Milady,' ignoring Damien altogether.

The queen went in and said to somebody who was still invisible to Damien, 'Roisin, I've brought somebody to see you,' and she beckoned to Damien who followed her into the room. Ciara had disappeared up the stairs and Damien could now see the occupant of the room. It was what looked like an elderly fairy who was sitting in a comfortable-looking armchair with a book propped open on her lap. He looked around and saw she was, in fact, surrounded by books, the room being lit by a lot of candles with a beautifully-woven rug on the floor. It had no windows but it all looked very cosy and was lovely and warm. He bowed to her and said, 'My name's Damien and I've come to talk to you about your religion if I may.'

She replied, 'I know who you are, young man, and I would be very happy to talk to you. I wondered if you'd be coming to visit me.'

'Thank you,' said Damien simply.

'I think you can leave us now, Gwendolyn. I feel quite safe with Damien.'

'All right, Roisin. See you soon. Bye.' And she turned and left.

So the queen had a name, Gwendolyn, Damien thought to himself and now he knew it, even if he wasn't allowed to use it, he felt more in control of things. 'Come and sit next to me. I'm sorry the chairs are so low for your large frame,' Roisin said now and Damien did as he was bidden. 'Now what do you want to ask me?'

Straight to the point, I like this old lady, Damien thought but I'll have to be careful. There are clearly no flies on her. 'I wanted to ask you about the gods you worship,' he said. 'I figured that I would never be able to understand this society without some knowledge of what you believe in.'

'You do have a wise young head on your shoulders, don't you? I happen to agree with you completely on that. Well, perhaps I should start by saying that we fairies mostly worship goddesses who are important for our existence. We are a matriarchal society as you must have noticed by now and a peaceful one. We leave all the more warlike gods to the leprechauns. Perhaps the two most important we call Dagda and Danu. Dagda is, in fact, a God and the father of many of our Pantheon and Danu is our ancient Mother Goddess. She is also the Goddess of water and is always associated with nature. Brigid is another very important Goddess, her most important attribute being Goddess of fire but she is also Goddess of poetry, music, healing and agriculture, all things which are also very important to us. Another we worship is Cailleach who is the controller of the weather. And, perhaps in all fairness, I should add Morrigan who is our only Goddess of war but is also that of fate. I think that's probably enough to be going on with, don't you?'

'Yes, probably. Thank you very much for that. It's all very interesting. How do you spell 'Cailleach' by the way?' Damien asked, who'd been scribbling frantically in his note book. She told him and, fortunately, his shorthand skills were pretty good so he was able to keep up with her words. 'But it does beg a few more questions. For example, what is your idea of fate?'

'Well, we believe that every individual has his or her own time to die and there's nothing much we can do about it but this doesn't mean that we don't believe in the idea of free will which is, actually, an important tenet of ours. And, before you ask, we also believe that, when we do die, we will join the Gods and Goddesses in their heavenly realm.'

'And do the leprechauns believe in the same things?'

'Basically, yes.'

'That all seems pretty positive to me and a good way to live and die.' Then, after scribbling more notes, Damien changed the subject completely. 'I couldn't help but notice all the books you're surrounded by. What kind of books are they and what are you reading at the moment?' he said, gesticulating towards the book lying in her lap.

'Oh, this is just a 19th century romance, a genre that I'm particularly partial to. It's by a lady called Charlotte Brontë and it's called *Jane Eyre*. I wonder if you've heard of it.'

'Heard of it? I had to study it for my A levels. It's probably one of the most famous novels in all of English literature.' And this led them into a discussion of the book and, in particular, of Mr Rochester, and whether he was a good or bad man. Damien found her comments on it extremely perspicacious, considering her lack of formal education.

When they had exhausted that subject, Roisin said, 'You asked me about all the other books around here. Some of them are reference books that I need for my job here when I have to conduct the various annual ceremonies for the fairies and the rest of them are personal choices of books I have asked Ciara to get me from the library here.'

'Do you have any modern books in this library of yours,' Damien asked now.

'It depends how you define 'modern'. The most modern that I have read is probably *1984* by George Orwell which I actually found rather depressing.'

'Hmm. That came out in the 1950's, I think, about 80 years ago. And I agree with you about it being rather depressing although I don't think Orwell intended it to be a particularly happy book. Anyway, I think I've taken up enough of your time, Roisin. I need to start thinking about getting back to my accommodation. But thank you ever so much for talking to me. If I'm ever invited back again, I would love to do it again some time.'

'I have enjoyed it too, Damien. I love having somebody I can talk to about my books. I am really rather cut off down here from intelligent conversation.' This last sentence was said very wistfully to Damien's ears. But she finished on a more upbeat note, saying, 'You know where I live now and my door is always open to you. And I predict that you will be back.'

Damien got up now, put his notebook and pen away, and said 'I really hope your prediction comes true,' and after saying bye again, he left her sitting there.

When he went outside her room, he found Ciara sitting on her mat but she jumped up when he appeared and said, 'Did you have an interesting conversation with the High Priestess?'

'Yes, thank you, Ciara. Most interesting. She predicted I'd be back again.'

'Fine. See you when I do,' she said before disappearing into Roisin's room.

Now Damien ran up the steps to the top and went out into the courtyard where he looked up at the sky. It was very grey and looked like a lot of rain was coming. He didn't want to get stuck in the forest during a thunderstorm, that was for sure, so he ran up to Gwendolyn's (as he now thought of her) private quarters. There he told her he'd had a most interesting conversation with the High Priestess and said, 'Thank you very much for inviting me here, Milady, and I hope you will allow me to return. But now I'm afraid I'll have to leave you as it looks as if it might rain and I don't want to get stuck in the forest.'

She looked out of a window and said, 'Yes, I think you are right, Damien. How long can you stay in the area?'

'What day of the week is it? I promised my wife and daughter I'd be back by the end of it.'

The question made her laugh and she said, 'I have absolutely no idea what you call it. We don't use weeks, months and years like you, just days and seasons. Nothing ever really changes here. But you never told us you were married with a daughter.'

'I didn't think it was relevant. Do you want to see a picture of all of us?'

'Oh, yes, please!' she said sweetly.

So Damien got his wallet out of his pocket and took out a fairly recent photo of the three of them on a beach earlier in the summer. It was taken by a professional and showed his wife sitting on the sand and gazing down fondly at the baby in her lap, who was giggling, with Damien sitting beside them both looking down also at the baby. He passed the photo to her and she scrutinised it closely before giving her opinion. 'This is lovely,' she said. 'Your wife and baby are both beautiful. Does your wife have a job?'

'Thank you. I think so and yes, indeed. She's a midwife at a big hospital in the capital. When she's working, the baby goes to a child minder.'

'We could do with her here. She could probably give our own midwives some useful tips.'

'Are you inviting her here?' Damien said now with a grin.

'Why not? I presume she gets holidays?'

'Yes, of course she does. The evidence is in the picture.'

'Well, then....'

'Thank you for that. I'll give it some thought. And now I really must be going. But I'll see you tomorrow if that's all right with you.'

'Yes, by all means. See you tomorrow, Damien. I'll get my husband to show you the way back through the forest.' She did that and then very soon he found himself walking behind Finn back to Titan's camp, his mind swirling with possibilities.

Chapter 15

But then as they got close to the camp, Damien suddenly heard a prolonged scream as of a young human girl in a lot of pain and he remembered Owen's mother telling him the baby was due any day now. He called to Finn who was striding up ahead and said breathlessly, 'I wonder if Owen's mother is having her baby?'

Finn replied saying grimly, 'I wouldn't be at all surprised,' but he was sprinting ahead now and Damien found it difficult to keep up. However, it was not far to the camp now and very quickly they broke out of the forest into the big clearing. Damien noticed there were a lot of adults congregated around one of the huts and then, peering through the rain, realised that it was, indeed, Owen's. Titan was there and Finn started talking to him rapidly in Elvish and he was nodding his head as if to say, 'Yes, you're right.' Then Finn asked him another question and Titan, who'd noticed Damien by now, replied in English, 'Yes, that would probably be a good idea.'

Whereupon Finn turned to him and said, 'I must leave you now and go back to the castle to get one of our own midwives. She is a fairy, after all.'

'Thank you for bringing me. I'll be fine now,' Damien replied. Then he saw a wondrous sight. Finn was flapping his wings, presumably to get rid of the moisture from the rain, before taking off like a bullet until he was just a speck in the sky. Damien realised that that was the first time he'd actually seen a fairy fly and he was truly impressed. But then he had another thought: I'm actually going to be present at the birth of what is probably only the second half-leprechaun, half-fairy baby in all of creation and he sent up a quick prayer to his own God that all would go smoothly, remembering the trauma of his own daughter's birth. And this sparked off yet another thought: Whatever happened to my reporter's objectivity? He remembered his professor at university telling him that, if he was to be successful as a journalist, he should never get too close to his interviewees but should always remain objective. Oh well, he decided, I can only go with the flow and my own feelings.

So he had plenty to think about but he wasn't allowed to dwell on his thoughts too long as he realised Titan was talking to him. 'I'm sorry. Could you repeat that? I was miles away.'

'I said, this is another big day for us all and I'm glad you're here to witness it.'

'So am I, believe you me. I was just offering up a prayer to my own God that everything goes smoothly.'

'Thank you for that. Every little bit helps. We are all praying that it will be a simpler birth than Owen's, which was almost a disaster for both the baby and the mother.'

'Who's in there with her?'

'Just the doctor and our own midwife – oh, and her husband of course.'

But then Damien shivered, realising how cold and wet he was getting, in spite of his hood which he'd put up already.

Titan must have noticed this because he said now, 'It might be ages before anything substantial happens. Let's go back to my nice warm hut and have some tea. My people will come and get me. You won't miss anything, I promise. You can tell me all about your adventures with the fairies.'

'Thank you, Titan. That sounds wonderful.' So they walked back together and when they arrived, Titan himself made the tea but Damien didn't ask him about this domestic side of his, presuming that his wife was somewhere in the crowd outside Owen's hut. Instead he pulled off his wet jacket and boots and made himself comfortable in one of the little armchairs, which he now considered almost his own. Then Titan came in with the tea and Damien started telling him about his day with the fairies. It always helped him to organise his memories when he had an audience and he realised that Titan was probably the best (and probably only?) audience he could have expected, just sitting there and listening quietly. When he'd finished, Titan looked at him quizzically and said, 'Well, you certainly seem to have been a hit with them. I think that's what you say, isn't it?'

'You never cease to surprise me, Titan, with your knowledge of English idioms but yes, that's exactly what we say.' And Damien could see Titan almost preen with the compliment. But then he said, 'However, I'm not sure about being 'a hit'. But all the ones I talked to certainly seemed very friendly.'

'What you see is what you get, with both the fairies and the leprechauns. They can't dissemble like you humans.'

'I keep forgetting that,' Damien said humbly.

But then they were interrupted by one of Titan's men who burst in, all excitedly, and said, 'Come quickly, Sire,' before running out again. Titan promptly rushed out and Damien quickly pulled on his boots and jacket and followed him. The crowd had grown even bigger around Owen's dwelling but he was so much taller than any of the leprechauns that he could easily see what was happening over all their heads. Then he saw the leprechaun doctor who he'd met earlier come out holding a bundle which was bawling its head off. 'It's a girl,' she shouted in Elvish which was quickly translated by Titan who he was standing next to now, 'and very healthy too as you can hear.' And there was a huge sigh of relief from all the onlookers. Then she added, 'The mother will be fine but she needs to rest now. So why don't you all go on home. The excitement's over.' And the crowd all started drifting away, chattering happily to each other.

Then the doctor saw Damien and came over to him. 'Would you like to see the baby?' she asked.

'I'd love to,' he replied and she unwrapped her and Damien saw a perfect little girl with the webbed feet of a leprechaun and just the nubs of fairy wings poking out from behind her back. But the doctor quickly wrapped her up again and said, 'I'll have to take her back into her mother now.'

'Please give the mother my warmest congratulations,' Damien said.

'Will do,' she replied and she disappeared back into the dwelling.

Owen appeared just then and said to Titan, 'I hear I've got a little sister. Can I go in and see her now?'

'Yes, I don't see why not,' Titan said and he scampered inside his hut.

Then Damien looked at his watch and saw it was getting really rather late now – it was almost dark – but at least the rain had stopped and he said to Titan, 'That was incredible! But I really must be getting back to my accommodation now.'

'Sure. I'll get one of my men to take you through the forest. See you tomorrow?' Titan said.

'Thank you for everything, Titan. Yes, I'll try and be here by the same time.'

And Titan was as good as his word, finding one of his scouts very quickly, who took Damien back out of the forest. The rest of the day passed in a blur, getting in his car, driving to the pub, having a warm shower, changing and then going downstairs for a quick dinner. The landlady tried to engage him in conversation but he was not in the mood and she soon, thankfully, gave up. Then he went back to his room and rang Moira.

'What have you been up to today then?' she asked.

'Boy, have I got a story to tell you!' Damien said in answer. 'But I'd rather save it for when I see you.' And the conversation was soon over.

Then he knew he had to ring his boss, Luella, and that short chat went much as the one with his wife had done. After that, he knew he was too tired to do any typing up of his notes so he simply went to bed, although his mind was whirring with all his adventures of the day.

Chapter 16

In spite of the fact that he had been really tired the night before, he didn't actually sleep very well. His mind was actually much too active but he did feel reasonably rested and he got up early as usual. It was Thursday now and he knew he had to return to the capital the next day so he was determined to use it as profitably as possible. He didn't bother reading the papers as usual after breakfast but instead went over all his notes again and added the most important things he'd learned the day before. Then he decided to make a list of the really crucial things he wanted to ask Titan and Gwendolyn and was surprised to find there was only one thing on it. But he knew it would take a lot of digging to find out about that so he wasn't worried about having enough to ask.

The time in the pub went quickly and, before he knew it, he was driving back to the forest. He didn't pass any other traffic on the road and, when he got there, he promptly blew his horn, knowing that it was probably the best way to alert Titan's men. One of them immediately appeared from the underbrush and he was led silently as usual back to the campsite. There he headed immediately for Titan's dwelling and after knocking on the door, was told to come in by the growly voice he knew so well now. He found Titan surrounded by some of his men who he seemed to be giving orders to but they were quickly shooed out and he was left alone with Titan.

'Hello, Damien,' Titan said. 'Sleep well?'

'Yes, thank you and I have something important to ask you.' And he plunged straight into his question. 'I would be very interested to know what you can remember about 10 years ago when you managed to get rid of the humans who were trying to build an airport on your land. How on earth did you manage to do that?'

'Oh, that's a rather long story. But basically I had a lot of help from Gwendolyn and I think perhaps it would be better to ask her.' And that's all he would say on the subject.

'Ok. I will,' Damien replied, not wanting to push it. But his interest was now really piqued by Titan's reticence. He had been so open in answering all his other questions. So he went on and asked him more about the leprechauns' way of life until Damien felt he had a reasonably good handle on it. After all, it was a relatively simple lifestyle the leprechauns had but he was very impressed by how they seemed perfectly happy with it. Actually, if he was completely honest with himself, he was actually very envious of them. They didn't have any of the psychological baggage humans had to carry around and deal with all the time such as envy, ambition, and jealousy or even simple things like money worries, but were almost a perfectly functioning micro-society.

He felt sure that humans could learn a lot from them and, when he told Titan this, he laughed and said, 'Are you seriously suggesting that we should all become your teachers?'

Damien wriggled uncomfortably at the suggestion but said, 'No of course not. I was just thinking out loud.' But then he looked at his watch and realised it was later than he'd thought. He'd been talking to Titan for more than an hour. 'I'd better be off now,' he said. 'Especially if I'm going to spend some time with the fairy queen. Don't forget this may be the last chance I'll get. I have to go back to the capital tomorrow.'

'No, I hadn't forgotten. But remember that you'll have to come back to show us the result of your labours.'

'Oh, yes, so I will. I had forgotten that I can't just post you my article or e-mail it.'

'That's true. Well, Damien, I have enjoyed talking to you and I hope you'll have plenty of positive things to say about us. How long do you think it will take to write?'

'You can be assured of that. I'm not even sure whether I will be able to publish anything at all about your society. But I reckon it will take me at least a week.'

'All right. I'll make sure somebody's waiting for you every day after seven days are up.'

'Thank you very much indeed for talking to me at such length, Titan. I'm sorry to have taken up so much of your time.'

'That's quite all right. As I said, I have enjoyed talking to you. Now I'll just find someone to take you through the forest to the fairy castle.'

'Oh yes, there is one more little, tiny thing: I was hoping to be able to visit Owen's mother. Do you think that might be possible?'

'She's not here. She's been transferred with her baby to the castle so she can rest up with her own folk. But I'm sure if you ask Gwendolyn nicely, she'll let you visit her.'

'Ok. I'll do that.' And on that note, Titan got up from his chair and went outside but was back very quickly with one of his men. Damien shook his hand and said, in parting, 'I'll see you within two weeks then?'

'Yes, I don't see why not. Goodbye, Damien.'

Damien said bye and then went off trudging through the forest towards the castle, following carefully in the footsteps of his guide.

Chapter

17

After a rather damp start to the day, as soon as Damien left the forest and started across all the little fields, he noticed that the sun was starting to struggle out and he no longer needed to put his hood up. He looked up at the castle and was once again overawed by what the fairies had done to it to make it habitable. As before, when he reached the main gate, it swung open immediately and after thanking his guide, he made his way inside and was led up to the queen's private quarters by one of the fairy guards. There he knocked on the door and at once heard a silvery voice, which he recognised, say, 'Come in.'

The queen was sitting straight-backed on some kind of tapestried pouf, weaving something on a small loom. 'Hello, Damien,' she said. 'Come and sit down and watch. You might learn something.' So he sat on a nearby chair and watched her dextrous fingers working on a complex picture which was just starting to take form. Apparently she didn't need a pattern unlike humans as far as he knew and he was amazed by the speed of her stitching.

'What are you working on?' he asked.

'Oh, just a simple tunic for the new baby,' she replied.

'It doesn't look simple to me. It looks incredibly complicated.'

'That's probably because you're a man,' she said now, grinning up at him. But now she stopped working and turned to him. 'And what would you like to talk about today?'

'Yes, well. I do actually have one very specific question: How did you manage to get rid of the humans and get them to build their airport somewhere else? I asked Titan the same question but he refused to answer and said I should ask you.'

He waited with bated breath for her to reply and, after a few seconds' pause, she did, saying, obviously considering her words carefully, 'I'm afraid I had to go against my conscience and do something which we fairies consider very bad although I understand it's normal enough in your world. But I'd really rather not say more than that if you don't mind. If you really want to find out more about that whole episode, I suggest you ask Roisin. I know she kept copious notes on it and, if she decides to tell you, she will. I will say one more thing though: I honestly think it was the only way to get rid of them and I would do the same again if I had to.' And there she stopped.

Damien was disappointed by this reply but he had to accept it. What kind of 'bad thing' was she talking about? He didn't believe for a moment that she'd committed murder but he'd have one more go by asking Roisin and after that, if she didn't add any more details, he knew he'd just have to give up and accept that the whole episode would remain a mystery. He just said, 'All right. I'll ask Roisin. Thank you for your honesty.'

'Anything else you want to ask?'

'Only about a million other questions,' he said, grinning at her. 'One thing I would be rather interested to know is why I can't get any kind of signal on my mobile phone even outside the forest.'

'Oh,' she said, grinning now back at him, 'that's easy enough to explain. Titan and I came to an agreement many years ago that we would block all radio signals in and around the forest so that our young people wouldn't be tempted to use your technology here.'

'So you are doing it?' he breathed, amazed by her words.

'Yes, indeed. It's not very difficult – really just an extension of our ability to make ourselves invisible but taking up a lot less energy.'

'What! You can make yourselves invisible?' Damien exclaimed in wonder.

'Yes, we can. I keep forgetting for how short a time you've known us and how much you still have to learn about us.'

'But that's incredible!'

'It might seem so to you but to us it's just rather a useful ability which we have developed over countless generations. How do you think it's possible for us to infiltrate your cities so easily on the rare occasions we have to?'

Damien was completely lost for words by this revelation and said nothing but just sat there thinking. Finally he thought of a reasonably intelligent question. 'Have *you* ever 'infiltrated our cities' as you put it?'

'Yes. I had to go to the capital once to visit a certain Mr Doggett at his house. That cured me of all desire to sample any more of the 'delights' of your so-called civilisation,' she replied rather sarcastically.

'That would have been about the airport business, I assume?' Damien asked, wondering if she was at last prepared to open up about it.

'My, you are well-informed,' she replied, 'but I've been trying to forget the whole sorry affair for ten years and I don't want it raked up now. As I said, ask Roisin if you want the details.'

'Yes, I'm very sorry. It's just my journalist's curiosity working overtime.'

'That's all right. I have done nothing I regret as I told you. Why don't I take you down to visit Roisin now if you're so keen to find out more about it?'

'Thank you very much. I'd like that.' So, on that rather unsatisfactory note, she led Damien all the way down to Roisin's room where they met Ciara who'd been sleeping outside with an empty plate beside her. This reminded him that he was getting hungry but he chided himself for the thought, reminding himself that a true journalist would always put a good story above hunger. But he'd been so well looked after with all his bodily needs fulfilled that he'd almost forgotten what it was like to feel any.

Ciara jumped up on their approach, all flustered, saying, 'I wasn't expecting you back so soon, Milady.' But she knocked lightly on the door and was promptly told to enter. She went in, closing the door in their faces, which made Damien smile, but quickly came out and beckoned to them both to go in.

Chapter 18

They went in and immediately Gwendolyn said to Roisin, 'I've brought Damien back to see you again because he is interested in finding out more about how we managed to get that wretched airport built elsewhere. As you know I've been trying to forget about it for years now and still can't talk about it easily. So I'll leave you two alone if I may.' And she rushed out again.

'What a busy lady she is, isn't she?' she said to Damien, smiling. But then she continued, 'I know, however, what's troubling her and it's true that, as a neutral bystander, I am probably a better person to talk about it.'

'So are you prepared to tell me what all the secrecy is about? She only told me that she had to do something which went against her conscience but that she had no regrets about it and would do it again if she had to.'

'Yes, I will tell you but only on condition that you promise me never to write about it for public consumption.'

'Yes, I promise unconditionally. I only want to know for myself anyway.' And as if to seal the deal, he put his notebook and pen back in his pocket.

'All right. That's good enough for me. Well, basically, it all came down to money. She had to use Doggett's and

McManus' avarice against themselves. So she bribed them.' And there she paused.

Damien now jumped in, 'What did she bribe them with? I thought you fairies had very little money.'

'Yes, it's true. We have very little ready cash. But she had a very clever idea. We have a Treasury near here which contains a lot of gold retrieved from a sunken Spanish treasure ship by our forefathers many centuries ago and which we've never had a use for. So she used a small portion of that. Basically just what they could carry out in their pockets.'

Damien pondered this for a few moments and then said, 'Yes, I can see why that might have worked. But even Doggett must have been responsible to someone else. What, for example, did the Prime Minister have to say about this moving of a whole airport? After all, it was a very expensive and large development.'

'Oh, he just went along with it after some of Titan's men found what was actually a better alternative, which was cheaper and even more convenient for the city than the one here.'

'Ok. Now I understand. Thank you very much indeed for explaining all that to me. Did you know that Doggett is now in a hospice for senile dementia patients?'

'No, I didn't know that. But, according to Gwendolyn, he was a very bad man and I think he deserves a bad death.'

This remark rather shocked Damien but, on consideration, he reckoned that the fairies had been very badly treated by him and he could understand it. 'And what part did McManus play in all this?' he asked now.

'Oh, he was just Doggett's lapdog. He just went along with everything Doggett suggested.'

'Ok. Now I think I understand everything. Do you think I could get to see this Treasury of yours?'

'Probably not today unless you're prepared to ask Gwendolyn to come back and take you. You'd never gain admission if you just turned up by yourself.'

'Fair enough. I'll have to come back again anyway to show the fairies and leprechauns what I've written. Maybe I'll ask then,' Damien said, thinking out loud.

'You do that. Is there anything else I can help you with? I hope that we can talk about something happier when we meet again.'

'I hope so too. No. I think that's it. I'd better be off now.' And, after saying bye and thanking her again, he left her then and went back outside where Ciara was waiting for him.

'Do you know the way back?' she asked.

'Yes, thank you. I'll be fine, Ciara. Bye again.' So he left her and went back up the winding staircase to the top and emerged again into the large courtyard, thinking about all he'd learned. Then he looked at his watch and reckoned he'd missed the beginning of the fairies' lunch but he knew that wouldn't kill him. So he just made his way slowly back to Gwendolyn's private quarters and knocked timidly on the door. He heard her say, 'Come in,' so he went inside and found her with her husband just finishing their lunch. 'I was afraid you might have lunched with all the other fairies,' he said.

'We did consider it but Finn pointed out that we weren't sure when you'd be back so we decided to eat here,' the queen said before adding, 'So how did it go with Roisin?'

'She explained everything to my satisfaction,' he told her.

'Good. I'm glad.'

'There is just one more thing I wanted to do while I'm here: I'd very much like to visit Owen's mother to give her my personal congratulations and maybe see the baby again.'

'Oh, yes. Finn had told me you were watching outside yesterday when it was born. Was that an interesting experience for you?'

'Yes. Very interesting indeed, thanks, especially when I got to see the baby up close.'

'Good. Well, I don't see why not. I'll take you now if you want.'

'Thank you, Milady. Well, goodbye Finn and I'll see you again quite soon.'

'Yes, goodbye, Damien,' he replied.

So they set off to a different part of the castle Damien hadn't visited before but soon arrived at another door, less imposing than the one to Gwendolyn's private quarters.

'Wait here while I see what's going on,' the queen said and she slipped inside but soon came out and said, 'She's almost finished feeding the baby,' she said. 'By the way, I wanted to ask you if you appreciate now why I didn't want to talk about my experiences with Doggett.'

'Yes, I understand perfectly now, thank you, Milady. Roisin got me to promise that I wouldn't include any of our conversation in anything I wrote for public consumption.'

'Good. That's a big relief for me,' she said, looking indeed very relieved. And Damien himself felt relieved that their relationship now seemed to be back on its old friendly footing.

But then the door opened and Owen came out with a big grin on his face and said, 'She's ready for you now, Damien.' So he went inside the smallish room and saw the mother lying up in bed holding a bundle, with rosy cheeks and a big grin of her own on her face.

She greeted him warmly and he asked how she was feeling now that it was all over. 'Very relieved, frankly, that this one came out relatively easily,' she replied.

'I'm not surprised,' he said. 'I remember very clearly how traumatic my own daughter's birth was for me. God only knows what it was like for my wife. But I must say you're looking very well.'

'Thank you. But we fairies are fast healers. I'll be up and about in no time.'

'That's good. Can I see the baby, do you think?'

'Yes, of course you can. You can hold her if you want.' And with that she handed the baby over to him and he took it very carefully in his arms.

He looked down at the tiny face with the little crown of gold fuzz on top of its head and said with awe in his voice,

'She's truly beautiful,' before handing it back to her. 'Does she have a name yet?'

'No, not yet. My husband and I are still arguing about it. But we expect it to be named soon. We'll probably give it a human name like we did for Owen. What's your daughter's name?'

'She's called Sophie.'

'That's a nice name.'

'Yes. We think so. Well, I mustn't tire you out. I just dropped by to congratulate you myself and possibly get to see the baby. But I never expected to be able to actually hold her. Thank you very much indeed for giving me that privilege.'

'And thank you for coming to visit me. I like having visitors.'

The queen meanwhile had been standing behind him listening to the entire conversation approvingly, and now she said, 'Damien's leaving us now for a bit but I've invited him to come back with his wife and daughter whenever he likes. But right now would it be all right if I ask Owen to take him back to the leprechauns?'

'Yes, of course. He's been getting under my feet too much here anyway. But make sure, Owen, you're back by dinner time.'

'Thank you, mother, and yes, of course I will be,' Owen piped up now excitedly from the back of the room where he'd been sitting on the floor reading a book. But now he closed it and jumped up, saying, 'Let's go, shall we, Damien?'

Damien smiled at his childish enthusiasm but said, 'Why not, Owen? But let me just have a last quick word with your queen.' They were outside the room now and Damien turned to Gwendolyn and said, 'I wasn't sure if you were being serious about inviting my wife here which is why I didn't mention your kind invitation before to you since you made it but, if you are, I am quite sure she would love it here. So thank you very much indeed.'

'She would have to swear to keep us secret,' the queen said seriously.

'Yes, I know but I'm sure I could make her do that.'

'All right then. Why don't you bring her for a short visit when you come with your article?'

'I'm not sure if she'll be able to get away but I'll certainly ask her.'

'Good. That's settled then.' And she strode off, presumably to her own quarters.

Owen now asked Damien impatiently, 'Can we go now, please?'

'Yes. So, how do you feel about having a younger sister?'

'Excited. Just think of all the things I'll be able to teach her!'

And the conversation just flowed from that point. Damien had forgotten just what a precocious child he was and he treated him like an adult, which Owen clearly appreciated. They soon arrived at the camp where Damien said goodbye to Owen, saying he hoped to see him soon, and he ran off to play with his friends. Damien walked over to Titan's dwelling and, when he was invited in, Titan, who seemed to be working on some papers strewn about him on his desk, asked him how his afternoon had gone.

'All very satisfactory,' Damien said. 'I found out from Roisin what happened with Doggett and McManus and Gwendolyn invited me back with my family.'

'Amazing! I wonder how she's going to explain that to her Council. But she must have been impressed by your behaviour.'

Damien didn't reply to this remark but said simply, 'I need to get back to the pub. Can you organise somebody to take me?'

'Yes, of course,' and he popped out for a minute or two and called one of his men who was passing to take Damien back through the forest. Then he turned to him and said, 'Well, Damien, so I guess this is goodbye for a while. I'll have somebody waiting for you every day at the gate after one of your weeks is up. I'm really looking forward to seeing what you write about us.'

'Thank you very much for everything, Titan. And *I'm* really looking forward to finding our more about you all. One thing I'm certain of is that I'll have many more questions for you when I see you again.'

And he left him there and wandered back slowly through the forest, wondering if he'd ever learn the way by himself. He arrived at his car and got in and just sat there for a couple of minutes, trying to organise his thoughts. The first thing he knew he needed was food as he was really starving now and, when he got to the pub, he asked the landlady what she could give him to eat and reminded her that he had to leave early the next morning. She appeared a few minutes later in the bar bringing him a huge plate of ham, eggs and chips which he devoured voraciously. Then, feeling much better, he decided next to call his boss and told her he'd be back about lunchtime the next day in the office and she was pleased to hear this. After that, he called the airline and made sure his return flight was still available, which it was, and then he started typing up his memories of the day on his laptop. This took him some time and, when he next looked out of the window, he was surprised to see it was getting dark already. So he stopped and went down to the bar where he had a pint with some of his by now familiar old cronies, then had a quick supper before going back up to his room again where he had a nice, long shower. Now he knew that his wife would have put the baby to bed so he rang her and reminded her that he'd be back the next day at some time in the afternoon. She told him she was excited to hear all his news and rang off. He packed then and, after that, watched the news on TV before conking out in bed.

Chapter 19

Damien got up early and went downstairs for a quick breakfast before paying his bill with his work credit card and then set off for the airport. He gave back his rental car and then had a short wait for his plane which was on time and he was back in the capital by about 11.30. He got his own car from the long term car park and then drove straight to his office where he was accosted by many of his colleagues asking where he'd been. He managed to fend them all off by telling them that he'd just decided to take a short holiday, before going upstairs to see his editor.

Luella, needless to say, was in her office and greeted him by saying, 'So the conquering hero returns,' which sounded slightly sarcastic to Damien's ears.

But he replied, 'Yes, and have I got a story for you!' and he proceeded to summarise everything he'd done with the leprechauns. He'd decided not to mention the fairies for the moment, thinking she might just have a stroke if he brought them up too early. She listened intently and he finished by saying, 'Now I just have to write something for you which I'll have to go back and show them to vet within the next couple of weeks. But I'm coming to the conclusion that they deserve just to be left alone.'

'Is there no way you could write something which would be acceptable to them and which would interest our readers?' she said after thinking about his incredible story for a few seconds.

'Yes, possibly,' he replied. 'I've been thinking about it all the way back here. But can I go home now and do some more thinking?'

'Yes, I don't see why not,' she said. 'And I promise I won't tell anybody your story until you give me the word.'

'Thank you,' he said and left her wondering if she'd just wasted quite a bit of money on his trip while he was thinking about how lucky he was to have such an amenable editor.

So, after visiting the Accounts department where he turned in his receipts, he went on home which was empty as he knew it would be with his wife out at work and his baby at the child minder's. There he did a few household chores before having a decent lunch which had been left him by his wife and just needed a few minutes in the microwave.

Then he settled down in his little office with his laptop and started writing up his story. He already had a title for it 'Leprechauns alive and well in Eire!' and had decided on using a pen name as he didn't want any of his colleagues or rivals knowing that he'd written it. Oh yes, and most importantly, he had decided in the car on the way home not to mention the fairies at all. That was to be his secret! He was pleased now that he hadn't mentioned them to his boss.

After he'd started writing, he found it was actually easier than he thought it would be as he'd already decided on a rough format and the ideas and the style came quite easily. He knew he needed to use a different style from his usual one if nobody was going to recognise him as the author. It was just a question of making sure he avoided any of his most popular words and making the syntax slightly more complicated than he was used to. He reckoned it would take him no more than a few days to knock it into shape.

He was still working on it when his wife returned with the baby. They greeted each other ecstatically and he gave the baby a huge hug which elicited a frown from his wife who said, 'Be careful with her. She's not an adult yet.'

'Sorry,' he replied with a grin and she grinned back so he knew he was forgiven.

Then he said, 'When can we talk?'

'How about half an hour? That should give me time to put the dinner on and change Sophie.'

'Fine,' he said, 'I'll go back upstairs and do a little more work.'

When he came back down again, he found his wife sitting in their living room reading a nursing magazine and the baby playing at her feet.

'Hello again, stranger,' she said, putting down the magazine and patting the sofa next to her. So he sat down and gave her a big kiss to which she responded ardently. Then she looked at him and said, 'So tell me all your news. What's the big secret about it?'

Now Damien looked at her seriously and replied, 'Before I tell you, you're going to have to swear on whatever you hold most sacred not to tell anybody else about what I'm going to say. Not your friends or your family, nobody. I'm being deadly serious now. Do you think you could do that?'

'Now you're scaring me, Damien. But yes, I swear.'

'This *really* is important, darling. Are you absolutely sure because the temptation to talk to someone about it might become very great?'

'Yes, I can keep a secret if I have to.'

'Thank you, darling. I was hoping you'd say that. OK, well....,' and now he hesitated before plunging on. 'I know this sounds absolutely ridiculous and totally incredible but I've just come back from visiting two tribes of the indigenous inhabitants of this beautiful land, namely fairies and leprechauns!' And now he stopped completely, waiting for a reaction from her.

She burst out laughing and said, 'I hope you haven't completely lost your mind, oh husband of mine. But do go on. I'm all ears.'

'I thought you might react like that. Actually it all feels like a dream to me now and I can hardly believe it myself but it's absolutely true. I've got reams of notes on my meetings with them and they're what I'm writing up now. The leprechauns live in a large forest and the fairies just beyond them next to the sea in the most amazing castle. They're so isolated that there is almost no contact with humans and they're totally self-sufficient. The way I found out about them is really just pure luck. They actually did have contact with humans some ten years ago when the humans decided to build an airport on their forest which the fairies and the leprechauns had to dissuade them from. This information was supposed to have been kept secret for ever but, owing to a clerical error, it was released after ten years and I just happened to have sight of it before it was reclassified. And that was what made me travel all that way.' And there he stopped again.

'That's the most amazing story I've ever heard!' his wife breathed incredulously.

'Good. That's more like the reaction I wanted. Now do you believe me?'

'I think I'd have to meet them myself to fully believe it,' she said now thoughtfully.

'Well, I think you'll have your chance sooner than you think because we have all been invited back there by the fairy queen whenever we can go.'

'What! Even the baby?'

'Yes, indeed. I showed them the picture of the three of us I keep in my wallet. The one taken on the beach, you know, and they seemed particularly interested in the baby.'

'OK. When do you suggest we go?' she said decisively now.

'That's the spirit, girl. I was thinking next weekend as long as you're not working. We could leave on Friday evening and be back latish Sunday. I have to go back anyway and show them the article I will have written by then, hopefully.'

'I don't think I am, actually, but let me go and check my work diary.' And she got up from the sofa and he heard her dash into the kitchen. She came back a few seconds later, waving her diary and said, 'That should be possible.'

'Great! Pack plenty of warm, waterproof clothes. It can get very wet out there and quite chilly.'

'A real adventure!' she said now and he agreed saying, 'For you at least although there's so much I still have to learn about their societies.'

Then they all had dinner together with Damien fielding many excited questions from his wife about the two societies, and, after watching a bit of TV, finally went to bed.

Chapter

20

Damien had decided to divide the article into sections to make it seem more realistic. The sections were: Where they live but with no exact locations (which was to include their dwellings) / What do they look like? / What do they believe in? (which was based mainly on his talk with Roisin) / Their language, especially their written language, including their ability to speak English. (Based on his talks with Titan) / What about medical care? (to be based on his talk with the doctor) / What do they do for money? (Based on his talks with Titan) / A complimentary conclusion. He reckoned that this way he could always delete a section if it turned out too long for his newspaper. He had already finished the first two sections which were based on his own observation and the next day started on the third. It took him only a couple of hours to do that, rereading his notes to make sure he got the details accurate.

Then he broke for lunch and rang Luella to tell her of his progress and asked if he could finish it at home as he didn't want his colleagues peering over his shoulder at what he was typing. She told him that she quite understood but needed to know when he would be back in the office and he said that two more days should do it. She agreed to this and he was happy with this outcome.

So the next couple of days he was busy writing and editing his work. And, when he was finally finished, he breathed a huge sigh of relief. Then he printed it out and looked at it once more. It started: '<u>Leprechauns alive and well in Eire</u> by W. Rochester, Freelance Investigative Reporter.' (He'd based the pen name on Mr Rochester, the hero of Charlotte Brontë's novel, Jane Eyre, who he'd had such an interesting conversation with Roisin about and thought she might appreciate. Also he'd checked that no other reporter in Ireland had such a name which should have his colleagues scratching their heads in bemusement and he grinned at the thought.) The article went on: '*Is this a spoof or is it real? You decide.*' (He was quite pleased with these two sentences also as he hoped that the general reaction would be one of laughter, like his wife's had been, but it should provoke a lot of debate at least.) The first sentence of the article proper was: '*In a remote corner of our beautiful island there still exists a tribe of leprechauns and I actually had the enormous privilege of getting to meet the ones who are described in the following piece.*' (He thought it was important right at the beginning to have something very positive to say about them.)

Then he skimmed the rest of it and was pleased that it all sounded very realistic and plausible. And finally he came to the last paragraph which went like this: '*So it is an almost perfect and peaceful micro-society who just want to be left alone and, on that note, if any of my readers are tempted to try to find them, I don't think they have a chance in Hades as they are much too well hidden, even from the air. Also their forest is well protected by a large number of lethal traps which only they know the locations of. It was a huge stroke of luck for me to come across them and I am deeply indebted to their king for all his kindness while I was with them.*' (He thought this struck the right note of gratitude to Titan and warning to others who may want to seek them out.) So, on the whole, he mused, a good job done and he was looking forward to showing it to Luella.

When his wife came back, he showed it to her and her first reaction was, 'But you've never felt it necessary to use a pen name before, have you?'

'No, that's true but I felt that on this occasion it was essential,' and he gave her the reasons why, which she accepted.

Then she continued reading and, when she'd finished, she said, 'But you haven't mentioned the fairies? Why not?'

'I'd rather leave them out of it completely. I haven't even told my boss about them and, quite apart from their privacy, I think it would be too much for a reader to take in and they would simply decide that the whole thing was actually a spoof whereas what I wanted was to leave some room for doubt.'

'Yes, OK. I see your point. Well, I think it's well written and almost believable for the average reader. So well done!'

'Thank you, darling. Exactly the words I wanted to hear.' And they left it at that and started talking about the forthcoming weekend.

She began by asking, 'Where are we going to stay?'

'I thought we could just go back to the nice pub where I stayed last week. It's actually quite comfortable and I know the people there. Also they could use our business, I think. If that's ok with you, I'll ring them now. I just hope they've got a cot for the baby.'

'Yes, go ahead and do that. Just one more question: Who's going to pay for this little jaunt?'

He laughed and said, 'Always the practical one, you. I'll pay for it out of my savings. The newspaper has already paid for everything from last week. Just treat it as a short holiday.'

'You've really thought about this, haven't you? You've got an answer for everything.'

'Yes, well, somebody's got to, I reckon. Now there was something I wanted to ask you. Oh, yes, I remember now. The doctor at the camp told me she was fascinated by the idea of antibiotics. Do you think you could pack a few in your medical bag and bring that too to show the fairy midwives the tools of your trade.'

'Yes, sure. It's going to mean quite a lot to carry but all right. I thought, by the way, you could carry the baby on your back in our old baby rucksack. I know she's getting a bit too big for it now she's started toddling but I don't want her wandering off by herself into the forest.'

'Good idea! Ok. Anything else we need to discuss?'

'No. I think that's everything.' And that's where all the arrangements for the trip were left.

Then he rang the pub and the landlady was surprised to hear from him so soon. But when he'd explained about the beauty of the area and how much he wanted to show it to his family, she said she quite understood and booked him a room for Friday and Saturday nights, saying that she would put a cot in their room for the baby. He thanked her and hung up. Now he knew he had to book them flights which he did quite easily and then he rang the car rental company he'd used before and rented a small car for the weekend, telling them when he'd arrive and making sure they'd put a baby seat in the back for them.

After all that they had supper, put the baby to bed, watched the news and then went to bed themselves, his wife tired after all her exertions at the hospital and he because of all the mental work he'd put in during the day.

Chapter

21

The next day was Friday when they were due to leave for the other side of the country. They'd arranged to have lunch at home, his wife having got permission to leave work early, and Damien waved her off after breakfast. Then he went into work and called up to Luella. She was in as usual and asked him to come up. He went up to her office, armed with the one copy of the article he'd made, and found her working on the proofs of the next day's newspaper and at once just passed her what he'd written.

She read it intently and then said, 'This is really rather good, Damien, but why did you use a pen name?' So he gave her the same arguments he'd used with his wife the evening before about how he didn't want any of his colleagues or rivals pestering him for more details, which she also accepted just as his wife had. 'I don't see why we couldn't print this as a feature article in our Sunday supplement,' she said now pensively. 'I'm sure it doesn't break any rules.'

'That would be great!', he said. 'It's exactly what I'd hoped. You don't think it's too long?'

'Not for a feature article, no,' she replied. 'Now you can go back to your regular duties, I hope.'

'Yes, indeed. Are there any particular stories you'd like me to do some more digging on?'

Yes, there are. There are a couple of high profile corruption cases just about to start going through the courts. I suggest you liaise with Joe. He knows the details.'

Joe was the top investigative reporter for the newspaper so Damien knew now that it hadn't been a wasted journey, professionally speaking. He was definitely in Luella's good books! 'Yes, well, I'll certainly do that. However, I have to leave for the West at lunchtime today. I need to take it for the leprechauns to vet. So don't print it until I give you the say-so. And I intend to pay for the trip myself this time since I don't want to leave a long paper trail of receipts for anyone to follow. I'll be back in the office full time on Monday.' And there he stopped, having said everything he needed to say, he hoped.

'OK. There's no hurry on it. We can print it any time we want, I reckon, especially as I don't think you've got any rivals to the story. I'd like to show it to the owner of the newspaper if I may.'

'Yes, by all means do that. But don't let him grill you about who actually wrote it. I'm sure you can think up some kind of story to tell him.'

'Yes, of course. I know how much you want to keep this just between the two of us.'

'Indeed. Well, if that's everything, I think I'll pop back downstairs and meet up with Joe.'

'Fine. I'll see you on Monday bright and early.'

The conversation ended there and he left her on another high, knowing he could trust her. Back at his desk, he looked up Joe on his internal directory and dialled his number but he didn't seem to be in. Then he thought the most useful thing he could do was to reassure his colleagues about where he'd been, even if that involved him in a lie. But he didn't have to go looking for them as they came to him and he told them all the same story about taking a week's paid holiday with his family and then coming down with a bit of a cold which he didn't want to pass on to any of them. He even managed to cough realistically while he was doing this and they all accepted his explanation. Then he tried Joe again and this time he was in so he went to his office and there managed to get most of the essential details of the court cases he was due to investigate the following week and they divided up the work to his and Joe's satisfaction.

After that it was time to leave and he just went off home, satisfied with his morning's work. On the drive he made up a rather nice mixed metaphor about his work which made him grin: that, while the court cases were his bread and butter, the leprechauns and fairies were actually a big bunch of cherries on top. When he got there, he found his wife and baby back already. His wife was busy packing some of the baby's smaller toys and Sophie was watching a cartoon on TV. They had a quick lunch and then, after checking they had everything they needed, they set off for the airport.

The journey seemed to go very quickly for Damien and soon they were landing in the far west of the country. Then it was just a matter of getting the rental car, checking that the company had provided a decent baby seat for the back, and setting off on the last leg of the journey to the pub which they reached at about 6.30pm while it was still light. There they checked in with the landlady, who made a big fuss of the baby, and, after unpacking, they went downstairs to the bar where they had a decent dinner and the landlady had even found a high chair for Sophie.

Then they went back upstairs to put the baby to bed, watched some TV in their room and finally went to bed themselves.

Chapter

22

Damien spent most of the night worrying about how his wife would react to the fairies and leprechauns and she, needless to say, was too excited to sleep much. But at least the baby slept well even though she was in a strange cot. But still they got up with the adrenalin flowing and went downstairs for breakfast which his wife pronounced delicious, the compliment delighting the landlady who enquired where they were going that day. Damien told her that they were going to drive along the coast and stop wherever they felt like, which at least was fairly close to the truth.

Then they went back upstairs, changed the baby and generally got ready for their excursion, Damien making sure he had copies of his precious article in his pocket. He had tried to prepare his wife for the meetings by answering all her questions about the two tribes as best he could and adding a few more details of his own, including how the fairy queen had scanned his brain.

'Is she going to do that to me?' his wife had asked. 'I'm not sure I'd like that.'

'Don't worry. It doesn't hurt. I just hope you haven't got any secrets you want to keep hidden from her,' and he grinned at her.

'We've all got secrets, haven't we?' she replied. 'But, unfortunately, most of mine are ancient.' And she grinned back at him.

He was pleased with this humorous riposte as it meant she wasn't seriously worried about the possibility of being scanned and said, 'So are mine. I bet you mine are more ancient than yours.'

She'd packed all the baby's essentials in her capacious medical bag as well as the essential tools of her trade and they were soon ready to leave. So, after saying goodbye to the landlady with Damien telling her they had no idea when they'd be back, they all got into the rental car and drove off. Damien was pleased that the weather looked set fair with just a few high clouds in the sky. He didn't want her to see the castle first in the rain.

They got to the forest in about 20 minutes and Damien's wife looked about her in bewilderment. 'It doesn't look like much, does it?' she said, eyeing all the old equipment which had been left stranded there by the workers who'd tried to build the airport. 'It looks more like an abandoned building site.'

'Which is exactly what it is,' Damien said, looking at it freshly through her eyes. 'Now it's just part of their cover.' There was nobody around as usual which, of course, suited Damien down to the ground.

Then she noticed the high chain link fence which disappeared off in the distance on both sides and the warning notices which said, *'Private Property. Trespassers will be prosecuted.'* 'Well, that looks like a fairly daunting barrier,' she said now.

'Yes,' he replied, 'and that's only the first line of their defence.'

'They really are serious about their security, aren't they?'

'Yes,' he said but he wasn't really listening. He was more intent on beeping the horn of the car.

And almost immediately a deep voice answered, 'Is that you, Damien?'

'Yes, it is,' he said. 'I've got the article with me and I've brought my family for you all to meet.'

'Oh, really?' the voice said. 'I'm afraid, before I let you in, I'm going to have to ask the king if it's all right to let your family in as well. So please just wait there.' Then there was a rustling in the bushes followed by silence.

'Well, I don't think that was the friendliest of welcomes,' his wife said. 'But I was most impressed with his English.'

'Yes, but I thought I'd told you that some of them, including the king, really do speak it very well.' After that, they just lapsed into silence and sat in the car, waiting quietly. The baby meanwhile had fallen asleep in her car seat.

They had to wait about 15 minutes before anything else happened and then Titan's strong voice, which sounded a bit breathless as if he'd been running, came booming out of the forest, 'Damien, welcome back! I've got the fairy queen with me who had a premonition you'd all be arriving today.'

The next thing they heard was the silvery, clear sound of Gwendolyn's voice saying, 'I'm sorry about all this but we can't be too careful, Mrs Fletcher. I just have one question for you: Have you told anyone of our existence?'

'No, most certainly not! I swore to my husband that I wouldn't reveal anything about you all to anyone and I haven't! And please don't call me Mrs Fletcher. My name's Moira.'

'All right, sorry. That's good enough for me. Let them in, Titan.'

'Did she scan my brain? I didn't feel anything,' she whispered to her husband.

But there was no time for him to reply as they were suddenly confronted by the extraordinary sight of what seemed to be the entire male contingent of the leprechaun tribe and the fairy queen herself. His wife gasped in astonishment, much as he had himself when he first met them, and he realised that no amount of words or explanation could properly prepare someone for meeting them for the first time.

But there wasn't time for her to properly process the sight as one of Titan's men had now unlocked the gate and opened it and was gesturing them inside.

'Wait a moment. We still have to get the baby,' Damien said and he and his wife ran back to the car and opened the back door. While she was getting the baby out, Damien was putting on the child carrier and, as soon as they'd done that, his wife carefully put the baby into it on Damien's back, checked that the straps were tight and then grabbed her heavy medical bag. Sophie was grizzling a bit at having been woken up and taken out of the nice, warm car but then they were ready to set off.

The fairy queen led the way with Moira following close behind her, trying to step only in her footprints and keep on the narrow path as she had been told to do. Titan followed her with Damien just behind him and then the rest of Titan's men. After the usual confusing 15-minute walk, they reached Titan's camp and Moira gazed around her with great interest. But Titan was hurrying them towards his dwelling and his men now dispersed with a last lingering glance at Sophie. He called out for Dronfeld and asked her to bring the four of them tea. Damien meanwhile had divested himself of the child carrier and put it on the floor where Sophie promptly fell asleep again in the warmth. Dronfeld brought the tea and both Moira and Damien sipped it appreciatively while Gwendolyn squatted down to look more closely at the baby.

'I think she's beautiful,' she said.

'Thank you. We think so too.' Moira answered.

'I know she will be a big attraction for my fairies.' But there was not much Moira could say to that. So she just continued sipping her tea.

'Can we do the business first before you two melt in a puddle of emotion?' Titan said now humorously, a remark which made Damien laugh.

'I presume you're referring to this,' Damien said, pulling the article out of his pocket.

'If that's your article, yes, of course it is. We're both dying to know what you've said about us,' Titan replied.

'Would you like me to read it to you?' Damien said now, remembering what Titan had told him about the leprechauns' poor ability to read English.

Titan replied at once, 'Yes, please. I was going to suggest that.'

'Ok. There are, however, a few things I want to say first, the most important being that I haven't mentioned you fairies at all in it,' he said, gesturing to Gwendolyn, 'only the leprechauns. I haven't mentioned the existence of the fairies to anyone, not even my editor. The second thing is that I have tried to stick only to the facts of what I was told and my own observations without any comment on them and, naturally, I haven't revealed anything at all about where you live. Also, for the first time in my career, I have used a pen name. If I use any words you are not familiar with, just stop me, Ok? Likewise if I got any of the details wrong. I'll correct them on the spot. I know my editor is waiting anxiously to get the final version. Both she and I are hoping it will spark a debate about the role of the indigenous inhabitants of our island in our modern society.'

'Yes, that's all fine,' Titan said now.

And so Damien launched into it and was relieved to find that he had only made a couple of small errors of fact which he corrected in pen. When he'd finished, he sat back, finished his tea and waited for a final verdict from Gwendolyn and Titan. Meanwhile Sophie was just playing quietly on the floor with one of her toys, being supervised by Moira.

After a few seconds' pause while they digested it, Titan said, 'Yes, well, Damien, I think you've done an excellent job there.'

'Yes, I agree,' said Gwendolyn. 'I especially liked the line near the beginning, *Is this a spoof or is it real? You decide.*'

'So do you both reckon it's fit to print?' Damien said.

'Yes, I think so although I'd like to run it by my council this afternoon,' Titan said.

'By all means. I don't have an actual deadline when it has to be in but, if possible, I'd like get it all agreed before I have to go back.'

'When do you have to leave?' Gwendolyn asked now.

'We both have to go to work early on Monday morning,' Damien answered. 'Our plane leaves at midday tomorrow.'

'All right. I'll tell you what. Why don't you both come back with me to the castle now? We'll leave Titan to his ruminations with his Council. You can have lunch with us and after lunch I've planned a special surprise for you both. You'll still have some time before you have to go back to your pub to speak to any of the leprechauns you want.'

'Sounds like a good plan to me,' Damien said.

'I'd like to meet the leprechaun doctor who told Damien that she was very interested in antibiotics. I've brought a few to give her if she wants them,' Moira said now, almost the first words she'd uttered since she arrived at the camp although Damien had noticed her paying close attention to everything that was said.

'That was very kind of you,' Titan said. 'I'll certainly arrange for her to be around later this afternoon.'

'Thank you, Sire,' she said simply as Damien had instructed her to address Titan.

So they left Titan and started walking through the camp where many of the women were outside watching them shyly but not approaching. The children were another matter however. Many of them came running up to Damien asking questions, such as 'Is this really your wife and daughter? Can we see her?' and Damien was forced to stop and introduce Moira and Sophie who seemed fascinated by all the small ragamuffins she was surrounded by. 'Not now, children, but if Moira lets you, you may be able to play with her this afternoon,' Gwendolyn said.

'Does she have any toys with her? Can we play with those too?' one particularly brave child asked, a question which made Moira laugh out loud and say, 'Sorry, I only brought a few small things but you'll have to ask her. She's not very good at sharing things yet.' And the little ones scampered off happily to share their news with their parents. 'What lovely children!' Moira exclaimed to no one in particular.

Then they were approached by a group of older boys who Damien thought he recognised and, when they asked eagerly, 'Have you got your computer with you, Sir?' Damien knew he was right in his recognition. However, he had to admit that he hadn't brought it that day but promised that he wouldn't forget it the next time he came if he was invited. And the boys too left reasonably happy. Gwendolyn asked him about this exchange and he admitted he'd lent it to them to play games on while he went to visit Owen's mother. 'Oh, trying to corrupt our youth already, Damien?' but she said it with a grin which let him know he was forgiven.

Then they were in the forest again and both Damien and Moira had to concentrate on where they were walking so there was no more talking. When they broke out of the forest and could see the castle for the first time in the distance across the fields in the by now bright sunlight, the sight evoked an involuntary 'Wow! That's amazing!' from Moira.

'You ain't seen nothin' yet, babe!' Damien told her with a grin in a fake American accent and she grinned back.

Chapter

23

They crossed the fields and the drawbridge and came up to the huge front gate of the castle which swung open ponderously as they approached. A guard came out and said, 'We saw you approaching, Milady.' But he was eyeing Moira and Sophie suspiciously as he said this.

'It's quite all right,' the fairy queen said. 'These two are Damien's family and I have invited them in. They don't need to be searched.'

'If you say so, Milady,' the guard said and stepped aside to let them enter. So they went into the castle and quickly came to the great courtyard which elicited another 'Wow!' from Moira and which Gwendolyn crossed without looking back. Damien knew from where they were heading that they were going to the queen's private quarters and so it turned out. They walked up the winding staircase and went straight in where they found Finn reading a book. Gwendolyn introduced him to Moira and then turned to Damien and said, 'Is there anything in particular you want to see while you're here?'

'There are two things actually,' Damien replied, putting the baby down on the clean floor and stretching his back. 'The first is that I understand that making music is a big thing of yours but I haven't heard any yet and I'd love to.' And there he paused.

'That's easily arranged,' she said. 'Finn and I can give you a little concert if you like. And what's the second thing?'

'I'd love to visit your Treasury if that's at all possible. Roisin told me about it and how it was quite near her room and I'd also love to visit her again.'

She paused before replying, then said, 'Yes, I don't see why not. I'd have to take you down there myself. You've seen more or less everything else, I think, and I know you haven't got an avaricious bone in your body unlike the other two awful humans who have been the only others of your species to have visited it.' And she shuddered at the memory before continuing, 'I bet Moira would also enjoy seeing it.'

'Only if it's not too much trouble,' Damien said.

'Yes, indeed. That would be really interesting,' Moira said now, supporting her husband.

'Fine. That's decided then. Now then, is there anything else either of you would like to do first? Freshen up, maybe?'

'I need to change the baby now,' Moira said.

'Of course. Can I help you? Follow me.' And she led Moira, who scooped the baby up off the floor, and they went off to Gwendolyn's private bedroom.

Meanwhile Damien sat down and started chatting to Finn about the book he was reading. The two ladies were gone quite a while but they came back a few minutes later with Sophie looking (and smelling!) much nicer and happier now she had a clean nappy on. 'That was most interesting for me,' Gwendolyn told her husband. 'It was the first time I'd seen a modern human nappy. I was telling her about the kind of tree bark we use for our own nappies.'

'Yes, indeed. That was fascinating for me professionally,' Moira said. 'Sorry we were so long, darling, but I got intrigued by some of the scents the fairy women wore and Gwendolyn was telling me what was in them which was also fascinating.' And then to Finn she added, 'I also reminded your wife about how I was looking forward to meeting any of your midwives who are free to show them the tools of my trade and, hopefully, to see theirs as well,' and she rattled her bag to show him where she kept them.

'Well, I can see you two are going to have a very busy day. When would you like to hear our music?' Finn asked.

'What about right now if that's all right with you both?' Damien said.

'Yes, fine,' Gwendolyn said and she retrieved from a corner of the room an instrument which looked much like a small harp or lyre to Damien's unpractised eyes while Finn found a flute-like instrument in his desk drawer. 'Let's play them some of our party music,' she said. And after a few seconds tuning up they started playing some of the most wonderful, ethereal music both Damien and his wife had ever heard. When they'd finished the tune, Moira and Damien burst into applause and Gwendolyn said, 'That's a dancing tune. We fairies usually fly while we dance together with our partners. But I'm afraid you'll just have to imagine that.'

'That was incredible,' Moira said softly, unwilling to break the spell. And Damien heartily agreed.

'Another?' Finn enquired.

'Yes, please,' they chorused. And they broke into another tune after a little consultation in Elvish clearly about what it could be. This one was equally moving and beautiful and the humans applauded long and loudly when it came to an end. Gwendolyn and Finn bowed to them and Finn said, 'Those are two of our party pieces which we've only played before for a few leprechaun guests.'

'We are deeply honoured to have heard them,' Damien said absolutely truthfully. 'I could listen to your music all day.'

'That, I think, will stay with me for a very long time,' Moira said and they suddenly both looked at Sophie who they'd completely forgotten about and who was copying her parents by trying to clap her hands. 'I've never seen her do that before,' Moira said now. She hadn't made a sound throughout the entire performance but now was just sitting there clapping with her mouth open and a seraphic smile on her face.

'I think she appreciated it as much as we did,' Damien said.

'We're glad you all liked it,' Gwendolyn said.

'Any time you want a contract with a recording company, just give the word,' he said now, trying to be humorous.

'I hope that's a joke,' the fairy queen replied sternly.

'Yes. It was supposed to be. Sorry. No offence was meant. It's just that, like I told you once before, Milady, you have so much to teach us.'

'That's all right. Forgiven and forgotten,' she said with a grin. 'But don't expect us to teach you anything in the near future.'

'No, I won't, I promise. But thank you very much indeed for the music.' He'd forgotten how prickly the fairies could get about contact with humans and swore to himself he wouldn't make the same mistake again, even in jest.

'No problem, Damien. We're glad you enjoyed it. Now I think it's almost time for lunch, my stomach's telling me,' Finn said, pouring oil on troubled waters, which was one of his specialities.

'Why are you always hungry, Finn darling?' Gwendolyn said to her husband now.

'Damien's exactly the same,' Moira said. 'It's something to do with male metabolism. But can I feed Sophie here first? It won't take long and it will mean she'll probably sleep through our lunch.'

'By all means, my dear. Is there anything I can do to help?'

'Well, it would be very useful if you could warm up her food first. It's not essential but she usually prefers it warm.'

'You're not still breastfeeding then?' the queen said now with real interest.

'No, we stopped that a while ago when she started on solids.' And she took a little plastic container of food out of her bag and passed it to Gwendolyn who sniffed it and asked what was in it. This provoked a fairly technical conversation about the feeding of babies which Damien tuned out of. But it didn't last long and he was about to turn to Finn to resume their discussion of his book when Gwendolyn asked Finn to ring the bell for a maid which he promptly did.

'Could you get this warmed up for the baby, please? Not too hot though,' she asked her when she promptly appeared.

'Certainly, Milady,' she said and disappeared but not without a long backwards look at the baby.

'One of the main perks of being queen is getting people to do things for you, I find,' the queen said.

'Yes, I can understand that,' Moira said, rather jealously Damien thought.

However, the maid appeared again soon afterwards with the by-now warm pot of food and Moira fed Sophie who gobbled everything up very quickly. 'Gosh! She ate that quickly! All the fresh air must have given her an appetite,' Moira said but Damien was wondering if they'd slipped some kind of secret ingredient into it but rapidly regretted the thought and chided himself for it. Anyway, even if they had, it would only be for the baby's benefit, he told himself.

Then it was time to go down to the big dining hall and face the assembled masses of the fairies so with Moira carrying the baby this time and Damien putting the few little toys they'd brought in his pockets, they set off for the short walk following the queen. Damien asked her on the way what kind of surprise she had in store for them but she only replied, 'Be patient. It wouldn't be a surprise if I told you now, would it?' and he had to be content with that.

Chapter 24

They arrived outside the large dining hall but didn't dither around with Gwendolyn marching straight in. Inside Damien heard his wife catch her breath as she saw all the assembled fairies who were talking quietly amongst themselves but they all fell silent when they spotted Sophie and Moira. The four of them went up to the dais at the end of the big room and the queen turned to face her fairies. 'I have brought not only Damien to see you today but his family as well. This is Sophie, his daughter, and Moira, his wife, so I hope you will give them both a real fairy welcome.' And the entire room erupted with noise which Damien recognised as the fairy equivalent of applause, with everyone flapping their wings. Then Gwendolyn said, after waving her arms for silence, 'Now let us eat.' And she proceeded to say the prayer in Elvish Damien had heard once before with everyone standing silently.

After that it was the cue for the maids to bring in the big tureens of soup and she showed them where she wanted them to sit on either side of her with Finn next to Damien and the rest of her Council arrayed next to them. The tureens were giving off a most beautiful aroma and Moira, after putting down Sophie and giving her her toys to play with, tucked in heartily. 'This is lovely,' she said to Gwendolyn although Damien found it difficult to hear her with the babble of conversations going on all around them and he soon gave up trying to follow their chatting and concentrated on his soup. It was as good as he remembered and he finished quickly, burping quietly in appreciation. 'Have some more,' Finn said and Damien couldn't resist it.

Then it was time for the second course and, after the maids had cleared away the tureens, they brought in a different kind of pie from what Damien had had before but it was equally delicious and he asked Finn what was in it. He thought for a moment and then said, 'I think you call them truffles,' and Damien was amazed, replying, 'I've never had truffles before. They are very rare in our society and very difficult to find. I think we use specially trained pigs to dig them out of the ground.'

'Really? That's interesting. They are quite a delicacy for us too but we can find them ourselves by their smell and dig them up.'

'I really do have to remember how acute your senses are,' Damien said in reply. But, not surprisingly perhaps, Finn didn't respond to this remark. Then he noticed that Gwendolyn was no longer sitting next to him and asked Finn where she had gone.

'Probably to organise your surprise,' he said with a grin but that was all he'd say on the subject.

However, she returned a few minutes later, seeming rather breathless, and said to Damien, 'Well, we're ready. Now I'd just like you and Moira to go outside the castle and look up at it. I've told the guards to let you back in once the show is over. After you've witnessed it, come back to the big hall, OK? We'll all be there.'

Damien had no idea what was going on but he said 'OK,' anyway and got up himself from the table, collected Moira and Sophie, and the three of them left the big dining room. They wandered down to the courtyard, crossed it and went outside the castle, being let out by a guard who said, 'Don't worry. We'll let you back in as soon as you've seen it,' but without specifying what the 'it' was. Damien and Moira were now completely nonplussed by all this secrecy. But they did as Gwendolyn asked and just stood there in the middle of one of the little fields looking up at the castle.

Nothing happened for a few minutes but then the most extraordinary thing occurred. The castle seemed to start shimmering in the pale sunlight and then, after a few seconds, seemed to disappear completely. 'What the hell's going on?' Damien muttered while Moira just stood there with her mouth open, not saying anything. Then, after a few more minutes, the castle solidified again and could be seen clearly once more. 'That was probably the most extraordinary thing I've ever seen in my entire life,' Moira said now and Damien had to agree.

'What did they do to the castle?' Moira asked.

'It was presumably some sort of fairy magic,' Damien replied, 'Let's go back inside and ask Gwendolyn,' ever the more down-to-earth one of the two of them.

So they made their way back inside the castle and to the big hall which Moira hadn't seen yet. She gasped at its beauty when she saw it, exactly as Damien had done. Was it really just over a week ago? He couldn't be sure of what was happening to his sense of time and this frightened him a bit. He was so used to being anchored in the real world that being thrust into a world of magic was very disorientating for him.

He noticed at once that it was full of adult fairies, all of whom seemed rather drained and a bit listless, not rushing about like they usually did, and not even paying much attention to the arrival of the three of them.

But then Gwendolyn was striding towards them. 'Well, what did you think of that?' she asked bluntly.

'I was telling Damien that it was the most extraordinary thing I've ever witnessed,' Moira said.

'And I had to agree with her. But how did you do it and why?' Damien asked.

'That's two very different questions. I remembered telling you, Damien, about how we could make ourselves invisible and how interested you seemed to be in this ancient power of ours. Then I thought to myself it was about time we had a full-scale drill of making the castle disappear, which has a very practical use for it, by the way. And that we could do it while you were here for your entertainment. You are probably the first humans ever who've seen it happen in practice.

And she paused here for a moment before continuing, 'So what is this practical use? Well, we have a trumpeter stationed during all daylight hours above the castle in one of the highest turrets whose only job it is to watch out for any ships at sea which may be coming too close to the land and able to see the castle clearly. If one does, he blows his trumpet which makes a very loud noise to our fairy ears but is inaudible to human ones to warn us and we all have to rush to this room and hold hands in a big circle and then concentrate hard which uses up a lot of energy, believe you me. Then the castle just disappears like you saw and, hopefully, the mariner just rubs his eyes and imagines he was seeing things.

It's always worked before. Does that answer your questions, Damien?'

'Yes. I guess so. So I guess it's another line of defence for you. And how long have you had this ability?' he asked now.

'Yes, exactly. To answer your question, Damien, I have no idea but hundreds of years at least, if not thousands.'

'Well, thank you very much indeed for your honesty and for showing us it.' And Moira echoed his words.

'Us fairies are nothing if not honest,' the queen said. 'Now come along. You both have a busy afternoon ahead of you, especially you, Moira, and I thought now might be a good time to show you our Treasury.'

They had to wait a minute or two while she gave her fairies a little speech in Elvish, presumably congratulating them on a job well done, and they all started to leave the hall, looking stronger now. Then the queen strode out, followed by Finn and the human family. She took them down to way under the castle until they arrived at a big door which looked as if it could withstand a battering ram and which she rapped on with an elaborate code. An old fairy face appeared around the door which opened slowly after a lot of locks were undone and said, 'Who is it?'

'It's your queen, Eloise,' Gwendolyn replied. 'I've brought a human family to see you and the Treasury. How are you?'

'Not too bad, Milady,' Eloise replied, 'but this is highly irregular.'

'It's unusual, I know, but it's not irregular. I have vetted both of them carefully and they are good people. Now can we come in, please?'

'Yes, of course. Sorry. Please come in,' and she opened the door wide.

'I was hoping you could give them the standard tour,' the queen said, walking in followed by Finn and the humans who were looking around goggle-eyed at all the gold and silver on display which was gleaming in the light of many candles. Then she introduced Damien, Moira and Sophie to Eloise.

Now that they had been introduced and accepted by her, Eloise obviously felt on much firmer ground and, after making a fuss of Sophie, started to tell them the stories of the various pieces which Damien and Moira listened to with fascination. Damien was especially interested in the story of the sunken Spanish treasure ship which he had already heard a short summary of from Roisin while Moira seemed to be more interested in the jewellery and examined but only by looking, she didn't touch anything. When they came to the Spanish gold ingots which were lying in a corner covered by a big cloth, Eloise removed it with a flourish and said to Damien, 'Try to lift one,' which he managed to do but only with some effort.

'Gosh. That's heavy,' he said.

'I know but I've read that pure gold is one of the heaviest metals known to man,' she replied. 'Now turn it over. Do you see anything on the back?'

'Yes, there are some markings which look like a seal of some kind and some writing.'

'Yes. That's the seal of King Charles V of Spain,' she said, 'whose treasure ship it was which sank nearby. We have other pieces in our collection with the same seal.'

'Fascinating,' Damien murmured. 'So all these are over 400 years old?'

'Yes, I believe so although I couldn't tell you exactly.'

'And you have just hung on to them in here all that time?'

'Well, we found them so we reckon they're ours.'

'Yes, I see your point. Well, thank you very much indeed for the tour, Eloise. It's been most interesting. Can I ask you a personal question now? Do you live down here all the time?' He had noticed her bed in a corner of the room.

'Yes, most of it except when I go upstairs to eat.'

'Well, thank you again. I think we can leave you in peace now.'

'I have a final question, Eloise,' Moira said. 'Do any of the pieces have a role to play in your society?'

'Good question. Actually, yes, some of them do. We use them on certain ceremonial occasions, especially the old Celtic stuff, but not the ingots obviously.'

'Well, I would like to give you my own thanks for showing us round,' Moira said. 'I found it fascinating and everything is so very beautiful.'

On that note they all left and once outside the heavy door which was now bolted and barred again, Damien said, 'Now, I would like to visit Roisin quickly and introduce her to my family.' So they made their way up a flight of the winding stone staircase and along a corridor until they came to a door which Damien recognised. In fact, it was easily recognisable because it had Ciara's mattress outside it. There they all stopped again and Gwendolyn tapped on the door which opened and this time it was Ciara's chubby face which peered around it.

'Oh, it's you Milady,' she said, flustered as usual. 'Give me a moment.'

So they waited outside for a minute or two until the door opened wide and she invited them all in. Roisin was sitting as usual in her armchair and she struggled up when she saw Moira and the baby. 'I thought you might be coming to visit me today with your family, Damien. So this is your beautiful wife and daughter.' And Damien introduced them with Moira bowing to her and Roisin shaking Sophie's chubby, little hand.

'We can't stay long, I'm afraid. Moira's still got to meet the midwives here and I've got a few things to do also.'

'It's very nice to meet you. My husband's told me a lot about you, all of it good, needless to say,' Moira said.

'That's a relief,' Roisin said with the flicker of a grin.

'I've just come to give you this,' Damien said. 'It's a copy of the article which your queen and Titan have said is good to be printed now. You can read it at your leisure but I really just wanted you to see the pen name under which I wrote it.' And he passed it to her.

She looked at the beginning, saw W. Rochester and said, 'Mr Rochester, from Jane Eyre, I presume?'

'Yes, exactly. I thought it might amuse you.'

'Thank you for that, Damien. It was a sweet thought.'

'You can put it in your library if you want or just tear it up. It doesn't include anything about the fairies, only the leprechauns.'

'I most certainly won't tear it up but will decide what the best thing to do with it is after I've read it. It could become quite an important historical document for our friends in the forest. And thank you for not mentioning us.'

'My pleasure. Now I really have to leave. Goodbye, Roisin but I'm sure I'll see you again if I'm invited back.'

'I *know* you will be. Goodbye for now, Damien.'

After they'd said their goodbyes and left, Gwendolyn said to Moira, 'I'll take you to our midwives now.'

'Sounds good to me. But I'll need my medical bag which I left in your rooms.'

'Oh yes, I'd forgotten about that. Let's all go back there then,' and she walked away with the others in pursuit.

Once back in the queen's private quarters, Moira collected her bag, changed Sophie and put her in her papoose on her chest and left with Gwendolyn to meet the midwives, leaving Finn and Damien alone.

'What do you want to do first?' Finn enquired.

'I was thinking it'd be interesting for me to visit this trumpeter of yours and see the ocean. Do you think you could take me up to him or her?'

'Yes, of course. That's easy,' Finn said and Damien followed him up the long, winding stone staircase to the very top. He was breathing heavily by the time he got there and thought about how out of shape he was. But the sea air outside soon invigorated him and the view of the ocean was spectacular. The ocean seemed to go on forever all the way to the horizon and there wasn't a boat to be seen. He supposed that the next stop was America. Then he looked over the side of the parapet and saw the jagged rocks far beneath and thought again of the extraordinarily private place the fairies had found to live with the impenetrable forest on one side and the ocean on the other.

Finn introduced him to the trumpeter and Damien asked him (for it was a male trumpeter) if he could have a look at his instrument. He showed it to him and he was amazed by how light it was, even though it was much longer than a normal human trumpet, and Damien thought it reminded him of the kind of medieval heraldic trumpet he had seen in films which was blown to signal the start of a jousting tournament. He asked what kind of wood it was made from but was told by the trumpeter that he only knew the word in Elvish, not in English. He turned to Finn for help who said, rather helplessly for him, that he didn't know the word in English either. So Damien gave up on that tack and asked a different question instead: 'Did you make it yourself?'

'Certainly not,' he was told. 'We have a professional instrument maker who makes all our instruments. It is very difficult to make a decent instrument.' So fairy society had, presumably, many skilled craftsmen who made things for the others. Another important titbit of information about it, Damien thought, to be set aside for later consideration.

It was turning out to be an even more complex society than Damien had realised.

He thanked the trumpeter for his time and followed Finn all the way down to the bottom in a very thoughtful frame of mind. 'Now what?' Finn asked.

'There are only a couple of other things: first, I would like to say bye to Owen's mother and possibly see her baby again and second, if you've got the time, I'd love to try and learn a few of the runes you use for writing purposes.'

'As long as you're not too ambitious, I could certainly help you with the second thing. However, the first is out of my control as I'm afraid she's returned to the leprechauns but I know you'll be going back to Titan's place later and you could always ask him if that's possible.'

'Oh, ok. I'll do that. But are you sure you don't mind helping me with the runes?'

'No, not at all. I managed to teach my own sons after all,' Finn said. So they went back to his rooms and he took out coloured pencils and several bits of paper. 'What would you like to learn first?'

'Just a few simple words,' Damien said. And he spent a happy hour or so learning the basis of the writing system which, as he'd suspected, was based, like Chinese, on ideograms or pictures which, in a very rough kind of way, reproduced the world around them. When he got tired, however, Finn suggested they stopped and said, 'You're a quick student.'

'Thank you,' Damien said simply in response. Then he added, 'I think it's probably because I have greater powers of concentration than a child.' He looked at his watch and saw it was later than he expected. 'Where's that wife of mine?' he said.

'Still chatting to our midwives, I expect.'

'We're going to have to leave soon,' Damien said now.

'Let's go and find them.' Finn replied.

So they went off to the infirmary where Finn suspected they were and he was right. Sophie was happily playing with her toys on the floor, totally oblivious to what was going on around her, while Moira was explaining the use of some of her tools and the small group of fairies listening were rapt with attention. But she stopped when the men came in and said humorously, 'Come to find out how your baby was born, Damien?'

'Actually I was coming to tell you that we'll have to leave soon.'

'Just give me a few more minutes,' and she carried on talking. But she was as good as her word and soon finished. Then she put all her things away in her bag and the assembled fairies all fluttered their wings noisily in appreciation of her talk. 'No, I need to thank *you* for showing me what you use and letting me into some of your secrets,' she said. 'Now I just have to see *your* methods in action.'

'You'll have to come back and we'll show you. Also thank you for bringing your beautiful baby to show us and showing us your tools,' one of the fairies said.

'Oh, that was easy to do. And yes, I look forward to that very much,' Moira replied.

Then she scooped up Sophie, put her into Damien's baby carrier, gave her one of her favourite soft toys to cuddle, and they were ready to go. Finn asked where his own wife had gone and the same fairy said, 'She's probably doing her tour of the castle before dinner.'

'Hmm. Yes, you're probably right. All right, you two, I guess you need a guide back to Titan's camp. I can take you if you want.'

'Thank you, Finn. That would be kind,' Damien said and they left the fairies there, all discussing something in Elvish, doubtless what Moira had been talking to them about.

'Shouldn't we say goodbye to the queen?' Moira said.

'She might be quite difficult to find now,' Finn said. 'Don't worry. I'll say goodbye for you and explain about you having to leave. I expect we'll be seeing you both fairly soon anyway.'

'Yes, I expect you will,' Damien said. 'But how can we communicate to let you know when to expect us?'

'I've thought of an answer to that. The leprechauns have a friendly solicitor who is sworn to secrecy. I'm sure if you write to him, he'll pass on the letter. Just get the details from Titan.'

'Thank you, Finn. That is most helpful.'

So everything was organised now to Damien's satisfaction and they left the castle for the time being but both Moira and Damien were sure they'd be back as soon as they could.

Chapter

25

As soon as they reached the camp, Damien said, 'Well, thank you very much for everything, Finn, especially the most interesting lesson. I can take it from here. You go back and enjoy your dinner.'

When they were alone, Moira asked him, 'What lesson were you talking about with Finn? Was he trying to teach you something?'

'Yes. He was teaching me a few of their runes which they use for writing.' But that was all he had time to say because they had arrived at one of the leprechaun dwellings where he knocked lightly on the door.

It was opened by a very bubbly Owen who said, 'Hello, Damien. I heard you were around. And who's this with you?'

'This is my wife, Moira, and my baby, Sophie. Moira, this is Owen. He is the one who first alerted me to the existence of the fairies. I was hoping to see your mother and introduce your new baby sister to Sophie.'

'Good timing, actually. She has just finished feeding her. Come on in.'

So the human family followed him into the warm hut where he saw Owen's mother just putting the baby down for a nap. 'Oh, hello, Damien,' she said brightly. But then Owen interrupted her, saying, 'This is the rest of Damien's family, Mummy, his wife, Moira, and his own baby Sophie.' There was no sign of his father but Damien ignored that, asking his mother, 'Have you given her a name yet?'

'No, not yet. We're still arguing about it.' Meanwhile Moira had put Sophie down on the floor where she immediately toddled over to look at the nameless half-fairy, half-leprechaun little girl. She seemed delighted to meet someone who was even smaller than her and said quite clearly, 'Pick up?'

'Those are two new words for her,' Moira said in amazement. 'I'll help you. Sit on the floor,' said her mother and Sophie obediently sat on the floor. 'Is it all right if I put her on her lap?' she asked the baby girl's mother.

'Yes, by all means,' she replied but she was watching her closely.

So Moira picked up the little baby from her crib and put her gently in Sophie's lap where she nestled quietly with Sophie watching her adoringly. Damien thought this would make a truly lovely photo but he'd deliberately left his mobile in the car to prevent just such a temptation as he was afraid of putting any pictures of the leprechauns or the fairies on any of his devices just in case they got hacked or his phone got stolen. The adults (and Owen) watched this approvingly for a minute or two and then Moira said, 'That's enough for now, Sophie. You can play properly with the baby when she's a bit bigger.' And she picked her up again and put her back in her crib.

'You promise, Mummy?' Sophie asked now and the baby's mother answered for her, 'Yes, I promise, Sophie,' and Sophie at once went up to her and gave her a big hug. 'T'ank you,' she said. She still couldn't pronounce her 'th' sounds very well. Then Damien said, 'Well, your baby seems to be very popular with Sophie.'

'Yes, she does, doesn't she? You must come back with her soon,' her mother said.

So they left after they had said their goodbyes and, when they were outside, Damien said, 'That all seems to have gone very well, doesn't it?'

'Yes, indeed. Just like the rest of the day,' his wife replied quietly.

****

Then they wandered off slowly to Titan's dwelling, each holding on to one of Sophie's hands and swinging her between them. Damien knocked and was told to come in so they did and found him working as usual on a big pile of papers on his desk, covered with runes.

'Ah! The intrepid explorers return! Just in time too. I was going crazy, trying to deal with all this,' Titan said, waving at the papers he was surrounded by. 'Did you have a good day?'

'Yes, it was brilliant, thanks,' Damien replied. 'I think there's just one more appointment we need to make. If you remember, Moira wanted to meet your doctor.'

'Yes, I hadn't forgotten. But surely you both have time for tea with an old man first?' And he didn't wait for a reply but called his wife and asked her to bring tea for all of them. Then he asked Damien and Moira to sit down and tell him all about

Just Leave Us Alone!

their day. So they started to tell him but quickly realised there was far too much to say and told him this. 'Just the highlights then?' Titan asked. So they explained about how they'd been permitted to watch the castle disappear and Damien told him about learning a few runes with Finn and a few of the other things they'd done. When they'd finished, Titan said, 'Sounds like you've had a pretty successful day then?'

'It's been absolutely marvellous,' Moira said.

'Good,' Titan said and then he called his wife again, thanked her for the tea, which was echoed by Damien and Moira, and asked her to go and find the doctor. She arrived quickly and, while she was talking animatedly to Moira, Damien took the opportunity of telling Titan what Finn had said about communicating with their solicitor to let them know when they'd be able to return. 'Yes, that should work,' Titan said, 'provided that he's still alive of course. It's been some time since we needed his services. But, if not, I'm sure we can come up with something. So you want his address?'

'Yes, please,' Damien replied and Titan went over to a big trunk in the corner of the room which appeared to be full of more papers, rustled around in it for a while, and then said a triumphant, 'Here it is!' and passed an old letter to Damien. It had a professional letterhead at the top and Damien copied down the name and address and passed it back.

Then Titan said, 'If you could also leave me your mobile phone number, one of my men could go into a neighbouring village which has a phone box and call you from there to firm up the arrangements. We have done this before although, again, it hasn't been necessary for ages.'

'Yes, of course, you can,' Damien said and gave it to him. 'That sounds an excellent idea.'

'So when do you think you might be able to return?'

'I'm honestly not too sure. I have to get back in harness and do the work I'm normally paid for. The next holiday we have will be Christmas but we have two sets of parents to visit then and I doubt if we can cancel those visits. After that, we usually take another short break in February to go somewhere warm but it should be possible then.'

'How many months away is February? Remember we don't use your calendar.'

'Oh, yes. Sorry, I forgot.' He did a quick calculation in his head and said, 'It's about seven months away.'

'So, it'll be winter and it'll still be cold. But never mind. If you can make it back then, you know you'll have a nice warm place to stay if you want.'

'Thank you very much, Titan. That's very kind of you. Oh and, by the way, I almost forgot. How did it go with your Council this morning?''

'Fine. I had no problems with them. I'm determined to make an honorary leprechaun of you, you know,' a remark which made Damien laugh out loud. Then he looked around to see where his wife had got to but she was nowhere to be seen and there was no sign of the baby. But Titan said, 'Don't worry. She won't have gone far,' and that was the signal for her to reappear.

'Where did you go?' Damien asked her.

'Just back to the doctor's place. I needed to change the baby and thought it would be easier to finish our conversation there.'

'Oh, OK. Are you ready to leave now?'

'Yes, I suppose so although I wish I could have stayed longer, Titan.'

'Me too. Damien and I were just discussing when you might be able to come again. He told me February was a possibility.'

'Hmm. Maybe. I can't see us both getting away before that. But we'll aim for that, if possible.'

'Good. We'll still be here,' Titan said. Then he added, 'Now I just have to find a guide to take you back to the gate.' And he left the big hut but returned with Owen a couple of minutes later. 'Owen says he'd love to take you back,' he said.

'Thank you, Owen. That would be nice,' Damien said. And so, after saying their goodbyes to Titan, they started walking back to the forest through the camp.

But then suddenly Damien heard a kind of swishing sound in the sky behind him and he turned to see what appeared to be a great white bird bearing down on them. He turned back to protect his family but then realised it must be a fairy and relaxed. Moira was staring at the sky, open-mouthed, when Gwendolyn landed beside them (for it was she) and said, rather breathlessly, 'I couldn't let you go without saying goodbye properly. I'm sorry I wasn't around when you left the castle today but I had a problem to deal with in the kitchens. However, Moira, I really enjoyed hearing you talk to my midwives about birthing and parenting in the human world or, at least, what I caught.'

'I really enjoyed talking to them and learnt a lot, Gwendolyn,' Moira said gracefully but truthfully.

'Have you made any decisions about when you might be able to return?'

'Well, we think possibly in February which is about seven months' time. I don't think we're going to be able to get away much before that,' Damien said.

'Finn told me you were going to set up a system of contacting Titan so we can be given some warning. Is this true?'

'Yes, we've just done that and I hope it works.'

'And I hope that you will seriously consider staying with us next time so you don't always have to be travelling backwards and forwards to your pub. I'm sure we can make things comfortable for you.'

'I'm sure you can. We will see but thank you very much for your kind invitation and for all your help today. I think everything went *very* well,' he said.

'Yes,' Moira added, 'especially for showing us some of your magic. That was incredible!'

'Oh, it was the least we could do for the first nice human visitors we've ever had.' Then she went up to Moira and hugged her. 'Now I must get back.' And soon she was nothing but a dot in the sky.

'Was I really just hugged by a fairy queen?' Moira asked her husband, totally dumbfounded.

'It looked like it to me,' he said jokingly.

Meanwhile Owen had been just watching and listening to all this but now he started hopping from foot to foot, obviously impatient to get going, so they let him lead the way out of the forest. When they got to the gate, he opened it with a key he'd clearly been given by Titan, and said in parting like a miniature seer, 'I just know Sophie is going to get on really well with my baby sister. So see you in a few months, Damien, Moira and Sophie. I'm looking forward to seeing how much you've grown, Sophie, and teaching you lots of things about the leprechauns and the fairies.' And then he just vanished back into the bushes.

So they just got into the car and Damien had to turn the lights on as dusk was rapidly approaching and he drove carefully back to the pub in silence, mulling over everything he'd seen and done that day. And, fortunately, Moira left him alone, lost in her own thoughts, while Sophie just went back to sleep in her car seat.

Chapter

26

When they got back to the pub, Moira had a quick shower while Damien fed Sophie, and then, as they were both starving, they went down to the bar and ordered a hearty meal which they ate quickly in silence, Sophie just playing under the table. After that it was back upstairs again where Moira put the baby to bed who was fast asleep within seconds, collapsed on the bed and said, 'Yes, well, I'm exhausted myself now but it's a lovely type of exhaustion.'

Damien grinned fondly at her and said, 'I'm pretty tired myself but before I can go to bed, I need to call my boss.'

'Ok, do that but can we talk for a bit before we sleep?'

'We'll have the rest of our lives to talk about today,' Damien replied. 'Why don't you get ready for bed and I'll join you sooner rather than later?'

'You're right as usual, O Master,' Moira said ironically, a comment which earned her a friendly slap on her rump from her husband, and disappeared off to the bathroom.

So he dialled Luella's number at the office, forgetting that it was Saturday evening already, and was told by the receptionist that she had gone home. So he rang her at home, got through immediately and ploughed straight in to what he had to say.

'Well, fortunately, the leprechauns OK'ed my text with a couple of small revisions of fact. Do you have a copy with you?'

'Yes, somewhere. Give me a moment,' and he heard her rustling through some papers, guessing that she was still working in her office at home. 'OK. Got it. Fire away.' Damien read out the revisions from his own copy which didn't take long and then she said, 'That's good. I'm glad they didn't ask for a complete rewrite, especially as I showed it to Lord C., who asked me not to change a syllable.'

'So our lord and master liked it?'

'Yes, very much but only from a profit perspective. He's hoping that the article will sell lots of newspapers and get syndicated abroad.'

'Yes, that's more or less exactly what I was hoping myself although I was hoping to start a real debate.'

'Well, I'm glad you're both singing from the same hymn sheet,' she said jokingly. 'And, by the way, on the same subject, he's agreed to publicise the article before it comes out and I've been given a very reasonable budget for that. Also, by the way, it's too late now to publish this Sunday. But there are no deadlines so we're not in a hurry and it's actually better this way as we've got time to publicise the article before it comes out.'

'Blimey! You're really pulling the stops out!'

'Yes, well, I happen to agree with him that it's got real potential, especially to be syndicated abroad. He tried to get me to tell him more about the source but I just said I had no idea who Mr W. Rochester was and that I got it in an envelope marked 'Personal' with a Dublin postmark in the normal mail.'

'Thanks very much indeed for doing that.'

'That's all right. It's called protecting one's sources. 'Oh yes, and one other thing I almost forgot: I've thought of a way to pay you without it going through the normal channels. I have a kind of slush fund which I only use rarely for occasions like these. So you'll be getting a cheque for the article after it comes out directly from me and then, if we manage to syndicate it, further money from me.'

'Thanks again. You seem to have thought of everything. There he paused before adding, 'Although I would have done the article for free.'

'That's my job and no comment on your second sentence. Now, I hope I can expect to see you back in the office on Monday, all bright-eyed and bushy-tailed and ready to start doing your 'normal' work again,' she said, putting the word 'normal' into clear quotation marks.

'Yes, you certainly can. Do you have anything interesting for me to work on?'

'Yes, but I think I told you about that.'

'Oh yes, of course you did. Silly me. So much has been happening recently I hardly know if I'm coming or going. I look forward to working with Joe,' Damien said, rather ungratefully to his ears but then he added, 'Thank you for that too.' Damien now knew with certainty that his persistence on the story had paid off both professionally and personally of course. Joe was getting on a bit and his job was one that he coveted and he thought that maybe one day.....

And that was more or less the end of the conversation and he turned and saw Moira standing in the door of the bathroom, listening. 'Did you catch any of that?' he asked.

'Only your end,' she replied. 'But it sounded from your responses like she's happy with your work.'

'Yes, indeed she is. Apparently I've come out of the whole thing smelling like roses.'

'Good and talking about smelling, you need a shower yourself.'

'Yes, I know. I'll do that now and then I'm coming to bed.' And, after showering, he collapsed into bed and slept like a baby all night with no worries to perturb him.

Chapter

27

He woke up, feeling invigorated and ready to take on all comers. His wife was still fast asleep beside him as was the baby in her cot. It was the first time, to the best of his knowledge that she had given them a completely uninterrupted night's sleep but then he remembered that she hadn't had her normal nap the afternoon before and he put her tiredness down to this. He looked at his alarm clock and saw it was already 8 am. They needed to get a move on if they were to catch their plane. So, after using the bathroom, he reluctantly woke up his wife who grumbled a bit at first but soon disappeared off into the bathroom herself with strict instructions to him not to wake Sophie. So Damien packed their things and then just lay down on the bed again and waited for Moira.

When she reappeared, they went down to the bar and ate a big breakfast while Moira fed the baby who had woken up by now. Then they paid the bill and, after thanking the landlady and promising they'd be back but not for a while, they set off in their rental car for the airport. While Damien was driving, they had their first proper conversation about the day before, focussing particularly on when they might be able to come back. Their plane was on time and they arrived in the capital safely and drove home in Damien's car. After that, they relaxed for the rest of the day, reliving their adventures with the fairies and leprechauns. Damien said one thing to Moira during this conversation which she particularly approved of.

'I've been trying to think of something that I can give Titan to thank him for letting me publish my article and I think I may have come up with the perfect idea. The leprechaun doctor told me that he used to own an Irish wolfhound which he was very fond of and which died a couple of years ago. How about if I gave him an Irish wolfhound puppy to bring up,' he said.

'That's a brilliant idea,' Moira said enthusiastically.

'Good. I'm glad you agree. I'll need to find out whether there are any breeders around here which have puppies for sale.'

'Ok. Do that,' she said.

The next day was Monday and it came all too swiftly but Damien went into the office and soon slipped seamlessly back into his old routine of long days working hard. But he found working with Joe was as stimulating as he'd hoped and he was determined to learn as much as possible from him. His colleagues commented on how happy he seemed but he just put it down to managing to get away for the weekend with his family and they had to accept this.

Meanwhile he was trying to find a breeder of Irish wolfhounds and, at last, after searching online and ringing lots of people, he found one some way out of the capital who had puppies for sale and he and Moira decided to visit her that Saturday. So they set off with high expectations and Sophie sleeping in the back in her car seat. The breeder lived on a farm in the countryside and she welcomed the family warmly. They went inside and the first thing she asked was, 'Is the puppy for you or is it a present for somebody else?'

'Unfortunately we both work full-time so we can't have a dog at the moment. It's actually for a friend of ours who's been incredibly kind to us,' Damien replied.

'Does he or she know anything about Irish wolfhounds and, for example, how much they cost to feed and how much exercise they need?'

'Yes, he had an Irish wolfhound for many years but the dog died quite recently.'

'That's good. I'd hate to give away one of my puppies to somebody who won't look after it well.'

'No, that won't be an issue. The only problem is that we're not going to be able to visit him now until next February.'

'Actually, that's fine by me. I usually hang on to my puppies until they're about six months old anyway to make sure they're not going to have any problems and to get them properly vaccinated.'

'That sounds perfect. Can we see them now please?'

'Certainly. Follow me.' And they followed her back outside to a large barn. Inside it smelt of animals and, in a corner, they saw a huge Irish wolfhound suckling some small puppies. Sophie got very excited when she saw them and rushed over to peer through the bars of their cage, before turning to her mother and saying, 'I want one, Mummy,' very clearly. This made all the adults laugh and Moira had to explain that she was very sorry but the puppy wasn't for her. Maybe when she was bit older…. 'That's what you always say,' Sophie said, very disappointed, which made the adults laugh even harder.

'Are any of them boys?' Damien asked, fascinated by the long-legged puppies. He'd never been around dogs much and was a bit disturbed to think he'd have to buy one for his daughter, even if it was eventually.

'Yes, there are two dogs and one bitch.'

'We'll take one of the dogs then. Our friend is a real man's man,' Damien said now.

'Ok, that should be fine. Your daughter can cuddle it for a bit if she wants.'

'Oh, yes please, Daddy,' Sophie said excitedly.

So the breeder took one of the puppies out of the cage and passed it to Sophie. 'Treat it gently now,' Moira said.

'Of course, I will!' Sophie said crossly.

'Let's go back to the house now and we can do all the business side,' the breeder said. So they all trooped back to the farmhouse where Damien was rather shocked by the amount he'd have to pay but he reckoned that the money from Luella should easily cover it with plenty left over. The last thing they had to do was inform the breeder of a date when they could come and collect the puppy, but Damien had by now organised a date in his mind and this was swiftly done. When they'd finished, they knew they had to go back but Sophie promptly burst into tears and Moira had to comfort her before they could get her back in her car seat.

On the way home, Moira said, 'Well, that all went rather well, I think. The puppies were really cute, weren't they?'

'Oh no, not you too,' Damien said, 'but yes, I agree with you,' not saying which part of his wife's sentence he agreed with and they left the conversation there.

Luella was as good as her word and did a great job of advertising his article every day in the paper and she even got some airtime on the radio to plug it but without giving anything away about its content except generalities. But then it was Sunday two weeks later, Damien's big day, and he walked down to his local newsagent and bought a copy of the paper. He read through the article as he sauntered home and was pleased to see it had not been tampered with at all with a huge headline stating '*Leprechauns alive and living in Eire!*' It covered two whole pages of the colour supplement and was even advertised on its front cover. Damien was very pleased with the way it had come out and reminded himself to thank Luella for everything she had done for it. He showed it to Moira when he got back and she was very happy for him, saying, 'Perhaps you are a proper writer after all,' which she said with a big grin to take the sting out of the comment.

When he got into the office the next day, the talk was all of the article and speculation about who Mr W. Rochester was which he kept well clear of, saying only, 'Well, whoever he is, he certainly knows how to grab the reader's attention. I thought it was interesting and quite persuasive,' two sentences which couldn't be argued with and were bland enough to turn attention away from himself. The article did indeed cause quite a stir in the capital and that night it was even mentioned on the local news with a couple of the older, more prominent journalists on the paper talking about it with an interviewer. Damien duly received a fat cheque from Luella which he used to pay off all his debts but the big payoff came when national and foreign magazines showed an interest in the story and it was even syndicated, after being translated, in a couple of influential European publications. However, it was never really picked up in America except for the National Enquirer which normally dealt in gossip about the Hollywood stars or conspiracy theories like alien abductions. But they circulated nationally and paid good money for it, and the owner, Lord C., was pleased by that.

After all the excitement of the article, Damien focussed on the two upcoming corruption trials and was even commended by Joe for the quality of his research. So everything was looking good for him but he was really just thinking about going back to visit the fairies and leprechauns again. Then Christmas came round again and the family went to visit both sets of their parents as usual. Moira had managed to take some time off in early February and that was when they were hoping to return. They knew it would probably be very cold but they prepared well with plenty of warm clothes for themselves and Sophie. Damien, after booking the flight tickets, surprised that he had to pay for one for the puppy, wrote to the solicitor friend of the leprechauns, giving the dates of their arrival and then he just had to wait for the telephone call from Titan's man. It came about a week and a half after he'd sent off the letter and he was told that they would be waiting for him on his arrival date. He was also asked if they wanted to be put up by either the leprechauns or the fairies and he said that they'd rather stay in the pub as they didn't want to give anybody any trouble.

So everything was organised at last and, after collecting the puppy which was rather big by now, they duly set off at the end of the first week of February. They arrived at the pub the evening before they were due to meet their friends at the camp and the castle to a rapturous welcome from the landlady who said they must really like that part of Ireland to come at that time of year. They agreed that they did but said nothing more to satisfy her inquisitiveness. After a big dinner they put Sophie to bed in her cot, turned on the baby alarm and went back downstairs to have a drink with the dog. There they met up with a few of the oldies who frequented the pub and had an interesting chat about the neighbourhood, Damien trying to glean as much of the local gossip as possible. After that they went upstairs, watched some TV and finally went to bed, excited about what the next day might bring.

Chapter 28

They got up quite late the next morning, had breakfast and then set off in their car to the forest. They were all bundled up warmly against the cold but at least the sun was shining although Damien had to drive carefully down the small road leading to the forest as it was very icy. When they got there, they found a reception committee of three including Titan, and a couple of his men, all of them barefoot as usual in spite of the icy conditions.

'Come quickly now,' Titan said gruffly. 'We don't want to be late for the party.'

'What party?' Damien asked.

'The queen has invited everybody to the castle for a big do to celebrate Brigid's day. She's one of our most important goddesses and one of the fairies' also.'

'Oh yes, I remember now. Roisin mentioned her. And we just happened to turn up on her day?'

'Actually, no. We normally would have celebrated it a few days ago but she postponed it in your honour. Brigid won't mind.'

'Gosh! That was nice of her.' But Titan was already striding away and Damien, who was carrying the puppy in a large cardboard box, had to run to keep up. When they got to the campsite, Damien knew he had to give his present to Titan now and he presented him with the box.

'What's this?' Titan asked.

'A little something from me to thank you for everything you've done for me,' Damien said rather breathlessly after his brisk walk through the forest carrying the puppy, which by now was quite heavy.

Titan peered inside and then gave a gasp of amazement. 'I don't believe it!' he said. 'Thank you so much, Damien!' and he gave Damien a huge hug which the latter was sure must have broken a couple of his ribs. And now he took out the puppy and let it lick his hand while his men looked on in astonishment. 'I think I'll leave him with the doctor who's still here,' he said, walking straight over to her hut and knocking on the door. She opened it immediately and was struck dumb by the sight of her king cuddling an Irish wolfhound puppy. 'He's a present from Damien,' he said in explanation. 'I hope I can leave him with you.'

'By all means, Sire,' she replied, having found her voice. And he passed her the puppy which she took in her arms where the dog nestled down, feeling perfectly safe.

Then Titan turned to Damien and said brusquely, 'Now, let's get on, shall we?' and strode off in the direction of the castle.

They walked quickly right through the leprechaun camp, which appeared to be deserted, and on through the rest of the forest until they came to the fairies' fields where they stopped to get their breath back and admire the stunning view of the castle which seemed radiant in the bright sunshine.

But they didn't dally and went straight across, noticing that lots of leprechaun and fairy children were playing in the playground, and up the crag to the main gate which opened as they approached.

They went on through, being directed by one of the two guards on duty to the big hall, from which a lot of noise seemed to be coming. Titan didn't hesitate, marching straight in, followed by Damien, his family, and Titan's men. However, Damien and Moira stopped on the threshold and just gawped at the amazing spectacle. There appeared to be hundreds of fairies all flying high above them, holding partners, but they quickly realised that they were dancing to the ethereal music coming from a whole orchestra of fairies seated on a dais at the end of the room. When the tune ended, the watching leprechauns all erupted into thunderous applause, stamping their feet on the ground, and Damien realised that must have been the noise they'd heard from outside. He and Moira clapped very enthusiastically themselves, even Sophie joining in although she was still strapped to Damien's back. But then they noticed Gwendolyn, who'd been dancing with Finn, coming towards them. Damien and his wife both bowed and suddenly the room went silent.

'Welcome back,' the queen said. 'How was your journey?'

'Fine thanks. That was the most amazing thing I've ever seen,' Damien said. 'I could watch all day.'

'So could I,' Moira added for good measure.

'We thought you might enjoy it although I hope Titan explained that every year about this time we have a big party in honour of Brigid's day and the coming of spring soon. So it wasn't only for you. But it's lovely to see you all again.

However, I think we have one more tune to dance to before the leprechaun band take over. Come and sit over here,' and she escorted them to an empty bench on the side of the huge room. 'We'll join you soon.' And then she signalled to the orchestra to strike up again and went off to join her husband who was chatting to Titan. They immediately started playing and this time Damien and Moira could properly appreciate the intricacy of the dance steps which the fairies were all following. But the music was equally wonderful, the harps and the flutes playing off against each other. When it was over, the leprechauns again started stamping their feet noisily while Damien, Moira and Sophie clapped until their hands stung.

After that it was time for the leprechauns to show what they could do and the fairy orchestra left the dais to them. Damien was fascinated to see that most of their instruments were drums, some huge, accompanied by a couple of other large instruments which looked to his unmusical eye a bit like double basses. Anyway, they had strings. Meanwhile Gwendolyn and Finn had joined them and the queen was quickly deep in conversation with Moira, leaving Finn to Damien who talked about books they'd been reading. Sophie, meanwhile, was toddling around the room being made a big fuss of by all the females present. But soon everything was set up and the new group of musicians started playing a wild dance tune which got all the leprechauns on their feet, stamping them in time with the music until the whole castle seemed to ring. It was very loud but very exciting to Damien who had Sophie sitting on his lap by now and who seemed to enjoy it also. He found himself tapping his toes along to the beat and noticed that Moira was doing the same.

When the amazing display finished, Titan made a pretty and mercifully short little speech thanking Gwendolyn for having them all and welcoming the human family to the festivities but also thanking Damien for the perfect present of the dog, and the fairies all fluttered their wings in appreciation while the leprechauns stamped on the floor. Then he said, 'Please can we eat now. I'm starving,' and everybody present burst out laughing.

'You'll have to wait a few minutes, I'm afraid, Titan, while we reorganise the room,' Gwendolyn said smiling at him and that was the signal for all the fairy maids to come in and set the benches scattered around the big hall up in long rows. At the same time the musicians left the stage carrying their instruments and within a short time everyone was seated again with the fairy queen and the leprechaun king sitting now on the dais surrounded by their most important ministers and the humans in the places of honour next to them. There was a roar of conversation in the room now but the humans were far enough away to be able to talk. Then, after Gwendolyn had clapped her hands for silence, Roisin stood up and made a short speech in Elvish, translated by Finn, thanking Brigid for another successful year and hoping that she would bring spring soon.

After that the food was brought in by the fairy maids and the leprechaun chefs and everybody started tucking in, Sophie being fed by her mother with her own food which Moira had brought with her. It was all delicious as Damien had expected and he ate everything that was put in front of him, including the portions of meat which he was served. However, he stayed clear of the ale which the leprechauns were drinking in copious quantities, sticking to water. Everybody was enjoying themselves, he could see, and he was pleased for Gwendolyn that the party was such a success.

But it was over all too soon and the leprechauns left with Titan telling the humans to be sure to visit him before they had to go. 'Is there anything special you would like to do now?' Gwendolyn asked them and Damien replied, saying that he would very much like to visit Roisin again, who seemed to have disappeared immediately after her speech, and also Owen's mother and her new baby. 'Easily done,' the queen said and led them down to Roisin's room where they found her surrounded by her books as usual and the remains of her own lunch which Ciara had brought her.

Damien bowed to her and said, 'It's lovely to see you again, Roisin.'

'It's very nice to see you too, Damien, Moira and little Sophie. Thank you for coming all the way down here to visit an old fairy. How's life treating you?'

'Very well, actually,' Damien replied. 'You probably heard that my article went down well with most of the humans who read it.'

'No. I'm afraid I didn't. But congratulations.'

'Thank you.' And he passed her a copy of it he'd brought with him, cut out of the magazine, telling her to add it to their library. The conversation flowed from there with Moira telling her how Sophie had caught a bad cold straight after Christmas but she was fine now and adding more details to what they'd been up to.

Then she said, 'I think it's time for her nap,' looking at her daughter who was lying on Roisin's bed and listening to everything they were saying while looking at the pictures in one of her old books.

'Well, thank you for coming again and I hope you'll be back soon.'

'Yes, we certainly will when the weather's warmer, probably during our summer vacation,' Damien said now and then they left.

On their way up the stairs Damien said to Gwendolyn, 'I don't think I thanked you properly for organising the party around us.'

'Oh, it was no problem. It was the perfect excuse to postpone it,' she replied.

Then they went back to her private quarters where Moira put Sophie down for her afternoon nap in her bed while the queen and her husband continued chatting to them and Damien gave them both a copy of the article to read at their leisure.

Gwendolyn said at one point, 'That was a most thoughtful present you gave Titan, Damien. I think it might give him a new lease of life.' And Damien was very pleased with her comment.

When Sophie woke up, they all went off to visit Owen's mother who they found in her room playing with the baby. Sophie at once asked if she could pick her up as she had before and before long she was dancing with her in her arms around the warm room while the adults caught up with their own gossip. The mother told them that they had named the baby Shivaun, an old Irish name which Moira thoroughly approved of. But then it was time to go and in parting the mother said, 'If you ever want to leave Sophie with us and go off and do your own things, please don't hesitate. She'll be quite safe here.'

'Thank you very much indeed. We'll certainly think about it,' Moira said, a bit nonplussed by this offer of free babysitting but recognising the truth in what she'd said. She would indeed be safe with the fairies.

By now it was the middle of the afternoon and they knew they'd have to take their leave so they bundled up again in all their warm clothes and left the castle after Gwendolyn had given Moira and Sophie another big hug with Finn guiding them this time back to Titan's camp. When they got there, he left them, saying, 'See you soon then for a longer visit next time. Maybe I can teach you more Elvish, Damien.'

'I look forward to that very much,' he replied.

They found Titan in his hut and spent another happy hour or so chatting to him with the puppy playing with Sophie at his feet and with his wife joining in much more freely this time. But this might have been because Moira was there, he thought. She seemed to have got over her shyness with the humans now. But when dusk was starting to fall, they knew it was time to go and took their leave of Titan and his wife, Damien remembering to give Titan also a copy of the article, which he was grateful for. Titan had already instructed one of his men to take them back to the gate and given him the key to the gate. They had an uneventful journey back to the pub, had dinner and went to bed, both of them very happy with their day.

Chapter 29

On their way back to the capital the next morning, Sophie was babbling away about her adventures with the fairies and drawing pictures of them in her colouring book and her parents were quite worried about her telling her school mates and teachers about them. So they knew they had to have a serious talk with her and, when they got home, Moira started by saying, 'Sophie, do you know what a secret is?'

'Yes. It's something you must never tell anyone,' or words to that effect in her toddler language.

'Very good. And do you think you can keep a secret?'

'Yes.'

'Ok. Good. Now what would you say if we told you that the fairies and leprechauns *must* remain a secret just between the three of us?'

'But why?

'It's too difficult to explain right now but when you're older....'

Damien broke in now and said, 'It's because they want to be left alone and if you tell anyone about them, they might disappear. You don't want that, do you?' Sophie shook her head, looking sad. 'Ok, so you must promise us that you will *never* tell anyone about them and that means anyone at all, not even your best friends or your teachers.'

'All right, Daddy. I promise.'

'Now promise Mummy.'

'I promise, Mummy.'

Then Moira picked her up, gave her a big hug and said, 'Good girl.'

And Damien added, 'This is *very* important, Sophie.'

'I understand, Daddy,' and it was his turn to give her a big hug. And that was pretty much the best they could do. Fortunately, they knew that she was highly intelligent and developing very fast. Now they could only hope.

So life continued for the Fletcher family. They used some of their new money to fly to a Caribbean island two days later for a few days somewhere warm and the rest of their holiday went by much too quickly, swimming in the warm sea and relaxing in their nice hotel. But too soon both the adults were back at work and Sophie later on started at kindergarten where her teachers all said she was precociously bright. As she grew up, they continued to take her back to visit the fairies and leprechauns where they could all be guaranteed the warmest of welcomes. The puppy had grown into a beautiful, full-size wolfhound by now, which Titan had called Max, and he was clearly training it well as it seemed to understand every instruction it was given. It was very gentle with the children, even letting them ride on his back, but Titan said it could be ferocious if ordered to be.

Damien progressed quickly with his knowledge of Elvish, even though he could see no earthly use for it in his normal life but you never knew, he told himself. After all, all knowledge was valuable. Also during this period, he decided to try to fulfil a long-held ambition of his and he asked Titan's and Gwendolyn's permission if they would mind him writing a fictional novel about them, stressing that it would be clearly marked as a fantasy, and they gave it. He spent quite a long time on this project, thoroughly enjoying the experience, and when he'd finally finished, he showed the manuscript to them and they agreed that it didn't reveal any of their real secrets, like where they lived. Finn said it actually made him laugh out loud in places. Then he just had to find a publisher for it and this was much more difficult than he had realised so, in the end, he self-published it and gave the first copies to Titan and Gwendolyn, giving away other copies to his friends and family. As a result, now he felt he could really call himself a 'proper' writer since he had finally written a book.

Moira meanwhile became very close to Gwendolyn, who shared her hopes and fears for the future with her, especially bearing in mind the encroachment on their land they had not too long ago experienced. And Moira told her a lot about the stresses of working in a big hospital and about how sad she was not to be able to have more children. She also helped out at several births for the fairies and leprechauns even though she found she wasn't really needed.

Then, when Sophie was ten, they reckoned she was old enough to be left with the fairies for most of the summer holiday while Moira and Damien went off on a long cruise, something they had always wanted to do. They got back to a very happy child who seemed to have learnt so much over the summer, including outdoor skills from the leprechauns, mainly taught her by Owen alongside his younger sister, and indoor ones by the fairies. She had also learnt some gardening skills from the fairies, so that was certainly counted a very successful holiday by them all. And she continued to go back at every available opportunity, which invariably mystified her school peers when they asked her where she went for her holidays. But she always managed to deflect the conversation onto firmer ground until she went away to university to study medicine where she was still very discreet. Nevertheless, in spite of how busy she was, she always managed to stay in contact with the two tribes, as did her parents.

Damien in the end did get Joe's job as Senior Investigative Reporter on the paper after he retired and was kept very busy at work. He still enjoyed the job but he never again wrote a story which affected him so much personally as the amazing experiences he had after that first meeting with the fairies and the leprechauns.

The End

Acknowledgements

First, I must acknowledge the huge debt I owe to my primary reader and good friend, Michael Black, who must have spent ages going over the manuscript with a fine toothcomb and saved me from multiple idiocies, both in my typing up of this book and also in the plotline. Then I would also like to thank another good friend, Hester Goddard, who offered several very constructive suggestions which I incorporated in the book. And finally, my thanks should go to the very professional team at my publisher's who produced such a good-looking book, especially June Tyler who coordinated the whole project.

www.ingramcontent.com/pod-product-compliance
Lightning Source LLC
LaVergne TN
LVHW021719060526
838200LV00050B/2748